MOIRA ASHE

KINDRED SPIRITS

BRENDON BERTRAM

ISBN: 978-0-9959812-5-6 (print)

ISBN: 978-0-9959812-6-3 (ebook)

Find out more at brendonbertram.com, on Facebook and at Goodreads.

CHAPTER 1

L ife follows the job.

That was Keegan Tait's creed. If you keep the job simple, your life remains simple. Let the job get complicated... well, that's why he only had two men left.

Keegan shuddered at the thought and shook his head clear, instead focusing on the scene in front of him.

He crouched amongst the long grasses to shield himself from the glow of the lone campfire that lit up the night a dozen paces in front of him.

The fire burned in a small roadside clearing—a perfect rest stop for weary travellers and an even more perfect place for a highwayman's trap. One such traveller was perched inside Keegan's trap, sitting on one of the makeshift log benches surrounding the pit. The fire outlined the traveller's dark silhouette and cast flickering orange ribbons over the foliage of the nearby treeline.

Keegan squatted in the tall underbrush and pulled on the collar of his green coat. Something about the figure bothered him. He strained his eyes against the darkness as he tried to squeeze more details from the traveller. He could plainly tell the clothes of the person were those of a man; a tricorn and a long overcoat. But beneath them, the figure was a woman's, of that Keegan was sure; no man had such narrow shoulders and such wide hips.

Keegan frowned. Women commonly disguised themselves as men on the road. He'd even seen a man travel by himself in the past month, a foreigner whose name he couldn't remember—"Doc," Keegan called him, for the medic's uniform he'd worn. What really bothered him about this new traveller was the fact that she was a woman travelling by herself. He shrugged his shoulders. Only one way to find out.

Keegan stalked towards the lone figure head-on. as he moved closer, he picked out the outline of a weapon lying beside her. A blunderbuss.

So she wasn't foolish enough to travel unarmed, Keegan thought. But it wouldn't deter him—he had faced much worse.

Pulling out his pistol, Keegan approached his victim. Nearing the end of the clearing, he stood up from the cover of the long grass and walked into the camp.

"Any room by the fire?" He asked holding his gun waist high but pointed squarely at his victim.

The woman rushed for her weapon, placing a single hand on it before freezing at the sight of the pistol.

"Don't even think about it." Keegan wagged the gun back and forth as he took a seat on the other side of the fire.

He looked into the face of the traveller as he settled into his seat. There wasn't much to see; a scarf pulled over her nose obscured most of her face while a scrap of clothing covered her left eye, leaving only her right eye exposed.

He studied the single dark eye staring back at him. He saw a lot in that flame-licked eye: loneliness, determination... but not fear.

This woman was a puzzle. Keegan smirked. His interest was piqued.

"As much as I would like for this to just be between you and me, I'm afraid I had to bring some friends." He turned away from the fire. "All right boys," he shouted, "let me know you're here!"

His buddies announced their presence with hoots and hollers, carelessly tossing their voices to create the illusion of numbers.

With a slight turn of her head, the woman listened to the commotion behind her. Keegan watched her narrow her eyes in concentration, trying to count the numbers no doubt.

"Eh!" he growled at her.

She returned her focus to him.

"All right love, nice and slow, let's see what you brought us today." He reached out his hand to her.

It took a few seconds for her to comply to his order, but she reluctantly lifted the weapon barrel-first and passed it over.

Keegan whistled as he examined the blunderbuss in the scant light. The thing was shorter than he'd expected but was well made—maybe too well made.

"Where did you get a weapon like this?"

"I found it," came the woman's muffled voice.

"What was that love?" He leaned the blunderbuss against the log beside him as he cupped his now-free hand around his ear. "Come on, take that thing off your face. I've been dying to see that pretty face of yours."

She eyed his beckoning hand before staring him in the

3

face once more. Pulling at the knot holding it firm, she threw the scarf with a flourish into the darkness behind her.

"Oh ho... I was definitely right about the pretty part."

The firelight danced along her cheekbones and down her slender face.

Beautiful.

She answered with tilt of her head. She lifted the hat off of her head, revealing shimmering dark hair. With a flick of her wrist, the woman sent the wedge spinning into the darkness.

"How about now?" she asked, smirking. Giving it the same treatment as the scarf, she flung the fabric covering the left part of her face aside.

The flames highlighted the horror show hidden beneath: the deep gorges carved across her face and that horrible, empty, sealed socket.

"Oooh..." Keegan whistled. "Sorry love, but all things considered, I've seen a lot worse." He wasn't sure if it was a compliment, but it seemed to draw a coy smile from her lips.

"How much worse?"

"A friend of mine fought in the navy. He was below deck when a cannonball was shot into his section of hull. The splinters tore half his face off. His chest was a mess and he lost his arm up to here." Keegan stretched his arm and used the butt of his gun to trace a line across his bicep.

He caught her eyeing his arm and saw her tense up. Keegan quickly withdrew his arm. Alarm bells went off in his head. Things were dragging on for too long.

"Show me what you got," he said abruptly. "Your money, now!"

She stood quickly and reached into her overcoat. He pulled the hammer back on his pistol, hearing the men hidden around them do the same.

"Whoa now... careful what you pull out of that coat there. Woman or not, we won't hesitate."

The smile never left her mouth as she slowly produced a pouch, which she casually tossed into his lap.

He let out a slight grunt as the heavy bag slammed into him. Keegan placed his weapon beside him as he pulled the pouch open. He dumped a small selection of coins out into the palm of his hand. Most of the coins were Fotland crests stamped with the Quinn coat of arms. So, she came from Quinn then—but more than one was an Abalonian crown. He let the heavy bag fall to the ground beside him as he plucked the silver coin out of his hand and held it up to examine, twisting it back and forth.

"You are a mystery that just won't be solved, aren'tcha love?" He held the coin for her to see. "Where did you get these?"

"From a friend. An Abalonian medic, in fact."

Keegan let out a hearty laugh. "Doc? Ha ha, crafty bastard told me he gave me all he had. Well, I guess this is when we part ways." He poured the coins back into the pouch and began to slide the blunderbuss over his shoulder.

"Don't you want to see what else I have?"

Keegan let the weapon slide back to the ground as he settled back into his seat.

"Show me what you've got then."

A playful gleam entered her eye as she unfastened her coat. Keegan's pulse began to quicken as she worked her way down the garment before letting the thing slide off her shoulder and fall in a heap behind her. The woman's hidden arsenal glittered.

"Eh! What are you playing at?" Keegan extended his arm, pointing his pistol at her.

She shook her head. "I just need to get rid of these." Her

5

eye never left him as her hands felt for the straps on her holsters. She let them fall off of her body before stepping out of the pile and around the fire, closer to him.

He stood as she approached, stepping backwards over the log. He ran his eye up and down her figure. Her loose shirt was torn, revealing her toned and scarred stomach partly obscured by a torn piece of fabric soaked through with blood.

She kicked her boots off into the darkness as she took a few steps towards him. Her eyes searched down him as well, lingering on his belt before rising again to meet his gaze.

A sickening crack broke him of her spell, but too late. She grabbed his extended wrist and pulled herself towards him. Pain exploded from his nose as he cursed.

"What the . . . ?"

She had an awkward grasp of his throat from behind him. He reached up and touched his injured nose, inspecting his blood as his two allies materialized in front of him, weapons drawn.

Keegan began to laugh as he felt the woman unfastening the rope tied around her waist.

"I don't have the foggiest idea what you're trying to do love, but you can let go of me now."

He began to bend over to retrieve his fallen pistol, but the woman yanked him upright with unnatural strength. He tried to pull away but she pressed herself against his back and held him fast.

The sound of snapping bone rose from behind him.

"Let me go. Do you hear me, let go of me." Keegan pointed at his crew. "Just go around and shoot this—"

He began to choke as the hand around his throat changed. He reached for the limb that grappled him. Panic rushed through his body as he felt her arm shift and reform itself beneath his palms. The woman's breath shifted from laboured gasps to snarls and growls.

Keegan tried to pull the horrid limb from himself, but she kept it tight. He struggled for breath as nails buried themselves in his skin.

He struggled to cry as he was lifted off the ground.

"Hee...llp... mmmeeeee!" Keegan wheezed.

His companions stood frozen, weapons limp in their hands.

Keegan couldn't even scream as a massive set of jaws tore into his shoulder. The woman, now a beast, flung him away, ripping the flesh from his body with her teeth.

He landed in the undergrowth. He didn't move, though steady convulsions racked his body—he only listened. He heard the gunshots. He heard the cries of panic turn to screams. He heard the beast as it tore his companions to pieces. Lying there, staring up at the stars that twinkled and shone through the treetops, he felt the heat drain from his body. His convulsions slowed and the pain faded as darkness engulfed his vision.

CHAPTER 2

It wasn't just the pinkish hue of the early sun that painted the soil red.

Moira stared at the stains on her hands. Dressed in the remnants of her would-be thieves' clothes, she sat facing the fire pit, a small collection of the bandits' supplies stacked beside her. A small wisp of smoke lifted off the still-smouldering coals, rising above the viscera of the previous night's events.

She'd wiped the blood from her skin a couple of hours ago, but the colour still remained. She could feel the faded crimson coating her fingers, dripping from her lips.

Moira clutched her legs to her chest as she buried her face into her knees. Fits over took her and she sobbed deeply, her cries muffled.

She didn't know what to do with herself now. She'd lost her home, her living, her reputation, the few friends who'd stuck by her. Maybe not Lincoln, but damned if he wasn't responsible for this mess.

A single moment had ended years of restraint. One taste awoke a craving long denied. She hated herself for relapsing, for breaking the promise she'd made to herself, but did any of it even matter? Anyone she met would likely kill her on sight once word spread from Quinn. Looking around, she wondered if it would be for the best. Maybe she really was the monster they all thought she was.

Moira's sobs faded and she leaned back against the log. She shook her head. They were wrong about her—she'd dedicated her life to protecting people. She'd risked her life to do it.

She still had her life, and with it she could rebuild what she'd lost. Maybe not in Fotland, but somewhere.

Qesuis seemed a good place to start.

The peasant revolt that raged there would make it easy for her to disappear amongst the chaos. Besides, it was the farthest she could sail before the next full moon.

It was horrible enough tearing the three highwaymen to pieces—it would be even worse changing while trapped on a vessel filled with people.

It wasn't a perfect plan, but she couldn't live in the wilderness alone. Death seemed like a kinder fate then that. So that would do: to Trident Bay, the closest port to Qesuis. From there, she'd sail into the country and disappear amongst the chaos of the revolution.

Moira wiped the tears from her eye and closed it, letting out a long breath before opening it again. She leaned over to grab a canteen before grabbing at her side as pain spiked through her abdomen. She fell back and pulled apart her coat, revealing her darkened gunshot wound.

The small flesh wound she'd sustained fleeing Quinn was still sore but was healing well, all things considered.

Without any medical supplies, it was a miracle that infection hadn't set in.

Covering the injury back up, Moira leaned over to pick up the canteen despite her wound's protest. She plucked the round metal container from the collection of stolen goods. Pulling the stopper out, she took a sniff.

Moira recoiled from the canteen as the brew stung her nose. She hadn't had a drink in decades, but if she'd ever needed one it was now. Taking a swig, she immediately spat it out. A miniature flare flashed into life as the liquid collided with the smouldering coals.

Moira coughed as the alcohol burned her mouth. She hurled it away, the container arcing through the campsite, drenching the ground beneath before coming to rest in the soil.

Moira groaned. Tilting her head back, she placed her hands over her face as another crying fit threatened to take over. Sitting there crying wasn't going to help her. She rubbed a fresh tear from her face and pushed herself to her feet. She squatted in front of the supplies and picked through them, taking only what she needed. A few bags of powder and rounds, some rations, and several pouches of coins. She eyed the rest of the canteens. Lifting the first, she pulled the stopper and smelt its contents. Smelling nothing, she took a cautious sip. Once the first drops of water touched her tongue, Moira tipped her head back, the neck of the canteen held firmly in her lips. She drank deeply. When the container was empty, she let out a sigh before releasing the canteen from her grasp, letting it fall to her feet with the ring of metal.

She left the weapons, the jewellery, and the collection of

trinkets—after all, her arsenal was hardly lacking, and coins were much easier to barter with than trinkets.

Wrapping her scarf back around her face, Moira pulled on her gloves and gathered up her blunderbuss. Slinging the treasured weapon over her shoulder, she walked towards the main road. Stopping by the alcohol-filled canteen, she looked down upon it.

That was one habit she really didn't need.

She gave the canteen a swift kick, sending the container flying towards the trees, spilling the last of its wretched liquid before bouncing off a tree with a resounding *bong*.

Moira strode away from the gruesome scene behind her.

From everything.

Towards Trident Bay.

CHAPTER 3

A ll of her life she had never seen the sea.

After walking for two days from her bloodied campsite, Moira stood on the southward road overlooking Trident Bay, marvelling at the sight.

The three long stretches of land that gave the bay its name thrust out into the navy seascape that glistened under the midday sun. Docks and warehouses covered the prongs of the trident and extended into the ocean, terminating at a wall that stretched across the seashore, splitting the wharf from the inland city that squeezed itself against it. Ships of various sizes crowded amongst the prongs and figures milled around, loading and unloading cargo. Finally, the ships glided wistfully out to sea, their masts bearing the heraldry of their owners.

Moira saw many stylized flags flying the colours of the famous H&E Trading Company. An enlarged "T" acted as a scale, balancing the "H" and the "E" perfectly. She saw the flags of Trident Bay's own fleet displaying two fish—one silver and one gold—swimming around a yellow trident. She spotted a multitude of others from various lands; some she recognized, others she didn't. Some ships flew no flag at all. But Moira's spirit swelled when she caught a glimpse of the roaring crowned lion of Qesuis.

Only one of the vessels flying the Qesuis flag was anchored at the bay.

Beyond the harbour, a stream of travellers entered and exited the city by roads leading south and west. One such traveller approached Moira as she stood admiring the view. His horse neighed and tossed its head to and fro, digging its hooves into the road as it neared her. It dragged a wagon of goods up the hill behind it. The driver of the wagon gave her a tip of his hat.

"Are the roads safe down south?"

Moira pulled her scarf up over her face. "Safer at least, but best keep your guard up."

He stroked his beard for a second before giving her a nod of his head. As he passed her by, he pulled the gun next to him a little closer.

She nodded back. "Safe travels to you regardless."

Moira used her finger to pull her scarf down and took one last deep breath of the salted air before pulling it back up. She then marched on towards the mass of wagons and carriages waiting for inspection.

Moira lingered amongst the crowd. She skulked through the masses, trying to peer into the rundown shack that served as a guard post. The guards looked more like fish-ermen then soldiers. Dressed in waxy yellow raincoats over brightly dyed wool jumpers, the men didn't seem to have a single piece of armour between them. Even some of the weapons they carried looked more like fishermen's tools; while the guards that milled around the crowd inspecting goods and people carried the common rifles and blades worn by other city guards, two men standing on either side of city gate carried hooked blades perched on the ends of wooden poles. Tall black hounds trotted anxiously between the vehicles, stopping only to inspect a wagon or traveller or when their master gave a tug on the leash.

Moira snuck her way through the crowd. A guardsman sat absently viewing the crowd, a collection of wanted posters pinned behind him. Moira moved forwards to get a better look.

She held her breath as she scanned the wall of sketched faces for her own. If she did find herself amongst the wanted, her options were limited. She could try sneaking in by hiding in one of the wagons, but the risk of being caught was too high. The guards might search them, and even if they didn't, she ran the risk of getting caught in the city. Her best chance would be to flee before she was noticed and try to find some other way out of Fotland.

Moira let out a breath when she found the wall vacant of her image. She composed herself and presented herself to the guard post.

The guardsman jumped from his seat as he spotted her. "Sir, you wouldn't happen to be a messenger from James-borough or Greengrove would you?"

Moira pulled down the scarf and shook her head.

The guardsman kicked the inside of the post. "Sorry ma'am, just haven't heard from them in a couple of days. Can I help you? If you don't mind me saying, you don't look well."

She wasn't surprised by his observation. She didn't feel

well. She was exhausted, and a ravenous hunger lingered on the edge of her mind.

"Thanks, but all I need is some food and some rest." Moira leaned against the counter. "Can you let me into the city?"

"Have you had any off your possessions stolen on your way to Trident Bay?"

She shook her head. "No."

"All right then, you'll just have to wait until your wagon is searched."

"I don't have one."

"You have a horse?"

"No."

The guard took a long look at the painstakingly rendered faces behind him before turning to face her again.

"Any weapons?" Moira twisted her body to show the weapon slung over her back and pulled open her coat.

"All right, all right." He rubbed his chin. "You should be fine with those as long as you keep them out of your hands. I can get you an escort to an inn if you like. It's a bit pricey, but it's the best place you'll find for comfort and food."

"I would appreciate that." She was starving.

The guard nodded his head. "Eh, Cromwell, I need an escort here to the Windwake!"

A large leather-faced man trotted up to her. A band around his arm bore a rearing unicorn—the heraldry of Skallond.

"This way."

Moira staggered through the mud behind him as the man strode alongside a carriage being ushered through the gate. She studied the sword the old warrior carried over his shoulder as it swayed with every heavy footfall. Atypical of those used by native Fotland soldiers, his weapon bore a much broader blade, one that was scuffed, dented, and stained from heavy use.

The crowds parted before her bright yellow escort as the soldier navigated their way through the rotting wood and crumbled stone of the city's old quarter. Cromwell paused as he heard Moira's laboured breaths.

"I'm okay . . . long journey . . . that's all," she managed between breaths.

He offered her his hand. "Here. Let me help you."

Moira grasped his hand, allowing him to put his arm around her as they walked together at a much slower pace.

"So . . . you're from Skallond?"

Cromwell let out a blusterous yell. "Aye! A proud one, or at least I was when there was still a Skallond. I came here with my wife and children over twelve years ago."

"Before or after the civil war ended?"

"After." He shook his head. "I fought in the War of the Twin Kings and I would have stayed whichever one ruled. It was the bastards from Abalon who made me leave my home." He spat into the filth at his feet. "Bastards all of them."

"Not all of them," Moira said.

The withered lines on Cromwell's face multiplied with his scowl. He replied with a snort. Moira felt his grip get slightly tighter around her hand.

They walked in silence out of the cramped squalor of the old quarter and into the slightly less cramped city market.

Moira could barely keep track of all of the colour and activity around her. People of every class gathered around an unending supply of stalls and shops. Merchants hawked anything and everything known to man: clothes, food, medicine, trinkets, weapons, live animals—if it could be bought, you could find it here.

Horse-drawn wagons waded through the river of consumers to deliver their goods to merchants. The crowd was filled with bizarre figures; a knight in full chainmail stood vigilant with a hand on his sword and a great burning tree emblazoned on his chest, and a figure shrouded by a hooded brown robe strolled the market, their face concealed behind a wooden mask. Bare-chested bruisers guarded the stairs to a brothel, armed with pistols and hammers. Beggars pleaded for money on their knees, thrusting their cupped hands towards everyone who strode by.

Moira yanked on her escort's arm. The old guard looked down at her. She gestured with her head to the tangle of beggars to their right. Spotting her target, Cromwell obeyed as they veered towards the dirty ensemble. Her escort released her from his grasp, allowing her to approach with a small pouch in her hand. Moira shook the pouch, making it jingle seductively. The poor masses became frenzied by her gesture. They crawled towards her—men, women, and children all crying and pleading at her feet. Hands outstretched and eyes filled with hope. One by one, she pulled out coins and laid them in the hands held out before her. The recipients wished blessings upon her, invoking the spirits and the creator and other religious figures before rushing to their feet and hurrying to join the crush of bodies surrounding the stalls.

A smile crept onto Moira's face as she was hugged by a boy, his coin clutched in his tiny fist.

Cromwell was tying the last remnants of his grey hair back when Moira returned to him.

"I didn't take you for a humanitarian."

Moira leaned back and crossed her arms. "Why not?"

Cromwell lifted his sword off the ground and slung it over his shoulder. He offered Moira his hand. "You're too well armed for a humanitarian."

Moira shrugged and accepted his hand. She couldn't argue with that.

They continued their journey through the masses, tracing the trail of wagons to its source. The crowds began to thin the closer they came to the city's seawall. A massive set of metal gates were left open, connecting the docks to the rest of the city and granting onlookers an arched glimpse beyond.

Moira and her escort entered the portal through the thick stone barrier. Once they entered the docks, Cromwell pulled her to the right towards a building easily four times larger than the warehouses that neighboured it.

The Windwake. Moira gawked at the monstrosity. Balconies circled the two-storey building, terminating in the front to allow a massive sign bearing the inn's name to nestle between the two ends. Patrons laughed and hollered outside, jostling and slapping each other, spilling their drinks into the soil below.

Cromwell released Moira and pointed to the structure before them.

"Go in there, get some food, get some rest."

Moira pulled another pouch from her coat. "How much for the escort?"

Cromwell waved her off. Without another word, he turned and strode off, still stroking his beard.

Moira called after him. "Thank you."

She heard a faint grumble come from the old warrior before he disappeared into the gateway.

Moira ploughed through the inn's double doors.

The scene inside was joyous.

Most of the patrons were gathered around a single table to her left. The group cheered and raised their bottles high every time a hoarse voice called for their opinions.

"Who wants another drink?" A parched voice asked.

The crowd cheered.

"All right, hey. Another round on me."

The crowd cheered again, raising their bottles high.

Moira followed the scent of food wafting from the kitchen. She squeezed past the line of girls carrying fresh bottles between each finger before leaning against the bar. A man sat beside her chewed on a plate of buttered potatoes and pork strips. It made her stomach turn and her mouth water. A bartender appeared in front of her.

"You want something?" he asked, leaning both hands against the bar. Moira couldn't tell if he was asking a question or stating a fact.

She looked up at her server.

"Damn, you look like shite, what happened to you?"

"I need a room, I need water—lots of water—and pork. Cook me up some pork and get this guy"—she grabbed the meat off the man's plate—"another side of strips."

The bartender nodded and took off to the kitchens.

The man beside her turned towards her.

"Hey, hey, thanks." Moira grabbed the meat off of his plate and began devouring the dripping strips.

"Oi!"

Moira tossed two coins into the man's lap.

The man pocketed the coins and returned his attention to his potatoes, poking them with his fork and muttering to himself.

Moira rested her head against the bar, lifting each piece

of flesh to her lips. Her hunger waned and her sickness dissolved with each bite, but the whispers remained.

She didn't even look up when the bartender returned, slapping a key, two cups of water, and a plate of roasted flesh in front of her face. She didn't look up when she handed a pouch of uncounted coins in return.

"Keep the rest."

There was no response, just footsteps.

Moira shut her eyes and pulled strips of hot meat off of her plate. Greedily, she tore the dripping morsels to pieces. She tried to listen to the conversations around her as she ate, but the raving of the crowded table nearest the door drowned everyone else out.

"Business is good, isn't it lads?" cried a voice.

"Yes!" was the unanimous reply.

"And who brings you that business?"

"You do!"

"I think we need another round over here. Hell, make it two, on me."

Another round of applause.

"Easy on the drinking, that's your sixth bottle. I don't want that . . . thing to take you from me." A woman's voice this time.

"What, the Terror of Trident Bay?" The voice answered. "Have you forgotten who I am? There isn't a sior-clan in all the world that could best me. No man neither."

The group laughed.

"I run this city, I protect this city, I make this city what it is. Who am I?"

The whole inn replied. "Caspian!"

Moira opened her eye. The name sounded familiar.

"Don't forget it. By the way, weren't you lads supposed to be working ten minutes ago?"

"Come on, just one more round!" cried another man's voice

The group agreed.

"Nope, no lads. Time to clear out you laggards. I need some alone time with this one."

A woman's squeal caused Moira to bolt upright and swing around in her seat.

Beyond the retreating curtain of workers, the owner of the parched voice was seated with one hand on a bottle and the other around a giggling waitress seated across his knee. The waitress' blonde hair cascaded off her shoulder, blocking the faces of the couple, but their bodies were exposed. The waitress' hand had probed beneath Caspian's clothes, splitting open his vest and shirt. Her hand massaged his chest, and although her touch looked soft, Moira noticed that it tensed with his every movement. Thin scars spread like branches across his chest.

Caspian's face burst out from behind the waitress. His stern head was shaven completely bald save for his eyebrows. He began to raise the bottle to his devilish grin, but paused mid-lift.

Moira froze as she realized he was staring back at her with his black eyes.

He raised the bottle—not to his mouth, but in her direction.

Moira turn back around in her seat. Quickly downing her water, she slipped the key into her pocket and pulled her scarf over her face as she headed for the exit, refusing to glance in Caspian's direction.

CHAPTER 4

M oira burst into the cool sea air. She kept her head down as she rushed towards the docks.

She slipped through the swarms of dock workers as they carried out their labours. None of them paid her any mind as she passed and none of the drivers acknowledged her as they drove by, but Moira felt comforted by their mundane hustle and bustle. She missed hearing the daily grind of others.

She was forced to slow her pace as she weaved her way through the stacks of cargo being loaded into carts and wagons.

The building thinned as she moved farther from the city, replaced by the masts of ships tied to the wooden posts that lined the prong.

People continued their work. A man cast a fishing line into the ocean while he dangled his feet over the dock. Past him, others loaded and unloaded ships, one of which bore a lion on its prow.

She ignored the other ships and marched on, unable to take her eyes off of the ship's gold and purple sails. She broke her focus as she neared the vessel, finally turning her determined gaze on the crew.

They swarmed upon the deck of the ship, tugging and tying ropes. A thin man watched the routine, stroking his well-groomed moustache.

"Hey!" Moira yelled up to them.

They continued unfazed.

"Hey!" She began slapping her hand against the hull of their ship. "Over here, hey!"

The captain glanced her way.

"Renaud," He spoke over his shoulder to a much shorter and heavier man resting in the corner. "Keep an eye on the preparations. We have a visitor."

Renaud groaned before hauling himself from the deck to lean against the ship's wheel. The captain strode to meet her, flinging himself off of the ship and landing next to her on the planks of the dock.

He bowed low, flourishing with a feathered hat with a brim as wide as himself. "I am Francois Beaufort, captain of *The Sunken Heart.*"

He used the oversized hat to gesture to the vessel beside them while he pecked the back of her glove with his lips. "What can I do for you?" he asked, speaking the common trade language in a heavy Qesuis accent.

"I need to get to Qesuis."

Francois dropped her hand and nodded his head. "Right you are Madame. We are headed back to Qesuis, but"—he replaced the hat on his head and tugged it down tight—"there is no way you will be sailing with us there."

"I can pay. Name your price and I'll double it." Moira pulled a pouch of coins out of her coat and held it out to him.

Francois gently brushed the pouch away. "It isn't about

money. Anyone caught sailing with unannounced travellers, particularly anyone from Fotland"—he gave her a wink —"will be charged with treason on account of Shaw and his 'hounds' giving the nobility so much trouble."

Moira dropped her arms, loosely gripping the small pouches in her hands. "I have no interest in joining Shaw's little group, or any of the revolutionaries. I'm just looking for a way out of here."

He squinted at her with a sideways glance. "I don't think the nobility will believe that madame." He pointed to the blunderbuss. "You look well-armed for a simple traveller."

"It's for protection."

Francois tapped a sabre hanging off of his belt. "This, madame, is for protection. That"—he pointed to the blunderbuss again—"is for spewing death. But the point is moot. It wouldn't matter if you were Antoine Leonce the sixteenth come back from the dead; there is absolutely no way you are coming aboard this ship."

"I need to get to Qesuis. Please, you have to help me." She dropped her coins and grasped the captain's hand in her own.

Francois closed his eyes and spoke in a low whisper. "I understand. My sister is a revolutionary. I've smuggled hounds in the past, but they've gotten wise. I've had too many close calls, seen too many friends marched to their executions." He wiped away a tear from her cheek. "I can't help you."

Moira nodded her head and released his hands. "Thank you for the information Francois, I'll try the other ships anyhow. Do you know of any other ways I could get to

Qesuis?" She picked up her coins while the captain vaulted onto the ship in one quick motion.

"None, but if you need to get there as desperately as you say, you'll find a way." He slipped his hand inside the stylish slanted opening of his jacket. "Good luck to you madame." He strutted back to his post and stood looking out over his crew.

Moira turned and left *The Sunken Heart* and her crew behind. She would find a way to Qesuis.

Every reaction was different. Some spoke, some shook their heads, a few even laughed, but the answer was always no.

Moira walked up and down each prong of the bay, asking everyone with a ship large enough to get her to Qesuis.

As darkness crept over the city, the people began to disappear, ships sailed away with nothing coming to replace them, and still Moira staggered up and down the docks.

She was left alone in the shadows cast by the orange sunset. She leaned against one of the many warehouses lining the docks. There had to be a way out of Fotland—she just had to find it.

Moira pushed herself off the wooden wall and continued her search, walking the narrow road towards the seawall with her head hung low.

"Well, well lass," A parched voice spoke. "You won't be finding the Terror of Trident Bay around the docks."

Moira stopped and looked up towards the voice.

A figure shrouded in shadow leaned against a board. A long-handled axe cut arcs through the air as the figure tossed it up and down.

The board they leaned against almost head-height. A

collection of random trinkets, scraps of clothing, and weapons were nailed to its face.

"What makes you think I'm looking for—what did you call it? The Terror of Trident Bay?" Moira replied.

"Truly? Moira Ashe isn't here to hunt the Terror?" The man chuckled. "And she don't even know what it is? Spirits help us all."

"How do you know who I am?" She slowly reached for a pistol with her right hand.

"The real question is what are you doing here if you're not hunting? Right?"

Moira clenched her left hand into a fist. She drew her pistol. "What do you want?"

The figure's hand stopped flipping the axe and gripped the hilt tight. "Whoa now lass, I didn't mean to scare you. I'm just curious is all. Here." He stepped out of the shadow and held his arms wide, not up in a sign of peace, but out so she could take in all of his grandeur. "I don't think I need an introduction."

Moira recognized his bald head, the sullen cheeks, those black eyes. "Caspian."

He gave her a nod of the head. "The one and only."

"What do you know about me?" She kept the gun on him.

He lowered his arms and looped the axe into his belt. "You're a hunter from Quinn. A few notable achievements."

"Is that all?"

Caspian tilted his head. "Should there be anything else?"

"Why me?"

"I don't know what you mean."

She thrust the weapon at him. "Why do you know who I am?"

He shrugged his shoulders. "I keep tabs on all the hunters around here. And, no offence, you are pretty . . . er, *unique-looking*."

Moira shook her head and stuffed the pistol back into its holster. "I . . . I'm sorry."

"No harm, right? Anyways, it'll take more than a shot from a wee pistol to kill me." He moved towards her. "What are you doing here?"

"I'm looking for passage to Qesuis."

"Truly?" he laughed. "Are you looking to become a revolutionary?"

She shook her head.

"Ha, well sorry lass, they aren't letting unannounced Fotish travellers there anymore."

Moira frowned. "I know. I've tried."

"But"—Caspian's laughter switched off in an instant—"I have a ship of my own. I could take you there."

"In exchange for what?" She closed the gap between them.

Caspian turned his gaze to the ground and began kicking stones with the toe of his boot.

"You don't strike me as a man who does favours for free."

"Hmmm, oh." He looked up at her again. "Well, it definitely won't be for free."

Moira loosened her grip. "How much?"

"I have more than enough money. I need a favour."

"What . . . kind of favour?" A sick feeling began to settle in her stomach.

Caspian used his hand to stroke the side of her face. "I can think of a few things."

Moira swatted the hand away and turned her back on him. "No deal."

"Wait a second lass. I just need you to kill something for me."

She faced him again. "Kill what?"

Caspian put an arm across her back and ushered her towards the board. "Do you know what this is for?"

"No."

"Every single piece pinned to this wall is from a different person, but they all suffered the same fate at the teeth of the Terror." He pointed to the board.

"There are over a hundred different things pinned to that board. Why has this gone on for so long?"

"Over a hundred here and growing." Caspian placed a hand on her shoulder and pointed to a collection of neck-laces dangling from the memorial. "I pinned those up not two hours ago."

"Whose were they?"

"Patrick Kavanagh and his two sons, plus their crew. They weren't the first but with your help they'll be the last."

She stared at the glittering fish chiming together in the breeze. Moira turned to Caspian. "The Terror, what is it?"

"It's a siorclan. Do you know what a siorclan is at least?"

She shook her head.

"A shark head on the body of a giant frog is the simplest description I can think of."

Moira crossed her arms. "Doesn't sound that dangerous."

Caspian laughed. "I suppose not, but just wait. The thing is tall as an ox with a mouth that could swallow you whole, but that's not how it'll eat you. It has jaws like a bear trap and half a dozen rows of teeth. If it gets its claws on you, it'll saw you into pieces."

"And why do you need my help?"

"I've killed other siorclans before, but the Terror is

different. It's not a mindless animal like the others—this one is a crafty bastard. I've almost killed it alone, but it's always escaped my grasp. That's why I need you."

"If I help you kill this thing, that's it, you'll sail me to Qesuis? You won't ask for anything else?"

Caspian smiled. "I don't think it'll be that easy, but yes, help me and I'll have my crew sail you there."

Moira gave him a sideways glance with her arms crossed. "All the other crews would be charged with treason if they tried bringing me into Qesuis, why are you different?"

"I know a couple of people there who owe me a favour or two." He held out his hand. "Do we have a deal?"

Moira eyed his hand for a few seconds before reaching out to shake it. "We have a deal."

Caspian gave her hand a single firm shake. "Perfect." "We'll start tomorrow morning." Moira rubbed her eye. "I need to get some rest first."

CHAPTER 5

I t was the best sleep she'd had in weeks.

It might have been the fact that her old bed at the Midnight Hour was rubbish, or that she'd been using a rock for a pillow these past few weeks, but Moira swore that the bed at the Windwake was worth every coin she'd overspent.

In spite of the siren call of her bed, Moira woke at sunrise and waited in the pub downstairs. None of the inn's staff had risen yet, leaving her seated alone near the door.

The first rays of daybreak shone through the large front windows of the establishment. Moira checked and double-checked her equipment as she sat in the empty room. She hadn't had the opportunity to use any of it since fleeing Quinn, but it was a necessary chore and was therapeutic in a way; it helped tame the pangs of hunger the hounded her.

"For the love of the spirits!" The bartender stumbled, still half-asleep, into the pub. "What are you doing here so early?" He yawned and stood looking at her through half-opened eyes.

"Food. Pork if you have it." She kept her focus on the glimmering knife she held in front of her face.

"Too bad lady, pork won't arrive for another two hours. The best we got is some chicken from yesterday, and some fresh mutton." The bartender shrugged his slumped shoulders and crunched up his round nose. "Well, fresh-ish."

"Is it already cooked?"

"No."

"Then I'll take the chicken."

"Anything with that? potatoes, eggs?"

"Just the chicken, thanks."

"Sure." He turned around and disappeared into the kitchen.

It took several agonising minutes for him to get back to her. When he finally did appear, he didn't wait for Moira to clear a spot on the table. He instead slid the plate in front of her, causing the dish to ring out as it struck Moira's equipment.

She gave him a threatening glare but he didn't notice. Instead, he disappeared as quickly as he'd appeared.

The chicken was cold but plentiful. Over a dozen slices of bird were piled up, some of the meat light, some dark.

Moira consumed the dish within seconds. It didn't quite hit the spot like the pork would have, but it was good enough.

She leaned back in her seat. Her equipment was in good order, she was rested, and she was fed. Now all that was left to do was kill a creature that had killed a hundred others. Piece of cake.

Moira reequipped her gear, left a few coins on the table, and left to meet Caspian.

. . .

"You look much better this morning lass," Caspian said with a wink.

"And you look . . . a lot less dressed." Moira looked at the bare-chested Caspian with a tilt of the head.

He stood defiantly in front of the memorial to the Terror's victims. His axe rested upon the strap of his suspenders, the only article of clothing he wore other than his boots.

"So I am. Can't do much fighting with your clothes bogged down with water." Caspian pointed the axe to her head and then dropped it down to point at her feet. "You might consider taking my lead. Don't know how useful you'll be with that thing on. If that thing gets wet, that's a lot of extra weight to be lugging around."

Moira placed her hands on her hips. "I'll pass."

"You say that now, but just wait." He began running his finger over the edge of his weapon.

"So where is this 'Terror' of yours?"

"Its lair is an hour's ride out of the city, in the bowels of Lane's Folly." Caspian kept his vision fixed on his axe, watching the light shimmer off its pristine edge.

"Shall we go?"

Caspian snapped his attention to Moira and looped his weapon onto his suspenders. "Right now? You don't want to get a drink first?"

"The faster I kill this thing, the faster I get to Qesuis. I'm already staying here longer than I wanted to."

"Do you really think it will be that easy?"

"Why not? With your knowledge and axe." Moira bumped up her shoulder and brandished her blunderbuss. "And my gun. This thing shouldn't stand a chance."

. . .

Moira fell forwards, planting her hands into the soft grasses that grew beside the jagged rock and upon the towering cliffs west of Trident Bay.

"Are you all right lass?" Caspian called. "Having trouble with the path, are you?"

"What path?" Moira hissed under her breath.

"What was that?"

"Nothing . . . just give me a second." She glanced behind her.

Trident Bay was an hour's walk behind them, and from here appeared miniscule. The tiny boats and carts continued to come and go, completely ignorant of their absence. Moira turned her head forwards again.

Caspian was looking past her, his arms folded in front of him, admiring the same view she'd just turned away from. He stood upon the sea cliff as sure-footed as the sheep that grazed and milled about them with blue belts died deep into their wool.

"Amazing city isn't it? When I first came to Trident Bay, it was nothing—just a bunch of rubble and rotten boards. I made that city what it is."

Moira pushed herself to her feet. "And how did you do that?"

"Hard work, planning, keeping what was useful." He looked down to her. "Discarding what wasn't."

"It sounds like fun," Moira replied, stumbling up the path to meet him.

"It still is; the work isn't over yet."

Moira did her best to keep pace with him as she tried to

33

mimic his quick steps. It took another half hour of walking and climbing before they came to the cave that sank into the ground.

Caspian waited for her, his axe firmly in his left hand. He stood in a stream outside the opening of the cave. Large enough for two horses riding side by side, the entrance was marked by a white creature painted onto a stone slab.

She stopped to brush the ferns away from the painting. "Is this what we're looking for?"

A pointed sail ran down the spine of the beast. Its nose jutted out above a gapping maw full of teeth, and its webbed fingers were tipped with claws.

"It's a bit crude, but accurate, more or less."

"I guess I'll see how accurate soon." Moira crept through the ankle-high water slowly, running her hand against the mossy walls of the cave as they narrowed into a darkness filled with the sound of roaring water.

"Are you ready lass?"

"Yes."

"Are you sure? This is the deadliest beast on the north coast."

"Not anymore."

Caspian clapped his hands together before breaking out in a smile. "That's the spirit lass. Come along now." He strode off into the opening and Moira followed close behind.

The pathway narrowed considerably as they moved deeper into the cave. Moira followed Caspian, darkness blinding her as they rounded a corner. After a minute, she began to pick out shapes again in the black.

"We should be getting close."

Moira could barely hear his whisper.

They crept slowly forwards. Caspian held his axe close

to him, while Moira kept her blunderbuss braced against her shoulder.

Something caught her feet, and she stumbled forwards, slipping on the wet stone floor. She cried out in surprise and tried to brace herself against the wall, but found nothing. She plunged downwards, landing far below Caspian in knee-deep water.

Moira choked and gasped for air as she pushed herself against the cold wall behind her. She grabbed her hat from where it floated next to her and slammed the dripping wedge on her head.

She called into the darkness above her. "Caspian."

There was no answer.

"Caspian."

"Moira? Are you all right?"

"I'm all right."

"Do you still have your guns?"

Moira shifted on her hands and knees through the water, looking for her blunderbuss. She gripped the weapon and held it against her chest. Water poured out of the end of the gun, carrying powder and rounds with it. The thing was useless now.

"Yes, but they're ruined."

"Shit."

"Caspian, do you know where this goes?"

"If you follow the sound of the water it should lead you to the main cavern. We'll meet there. It's going to take me a while though. If you find the Terror, run."

She had no intention of running.

Moira pushed herself to her soaked feet and looped the blunderbuss over her shoulder. Moira cursed and took several deep breaths in and out, but she couldn't stop shaking.

Fat grubs clung to the ceiling of the tunnel, their skin emitting a blue glow that sent spiderwebs of light reflecting off the water at Moira's feet to dance and shimmer off the walls.

Moira drew a knife and crept forwards, sliding her feet through the water while using her free hand to feel the wall beside her. Turning left and right, she blindly followed the sound of the river as she wound her way through the maze. The colony of grubs thinned out and she was abandoned to the darkness.

For several minutes, she saw nothing but inky black, heard nothing but the growing roar of running water and her own chattering teeth.

She stopped completely as her foot kicked the wall in front of her. She groped around for paths, but only found wet stone.

"Damn it!" She slapped her hand against the wall in front of her. Her own voice cried back to her from a hundred different directions.

A new sound froze her. A gurgle like a lung breathing in water echoed faintly through the darkness.

Moira gripped her knife tighter, her heart hammering in her chest. Her shiver worsened.

She stalked forwards, continuing to aimlessly navigate the labyrinth around her.

She froze again as she heard the sound once more and strained to discern which direction it was coming from.

The gurgle came again.

Moira shook her head. It sounded like it was coming at her from every direction. She took a deep breath and crept forwards.

. . .

A faint light shone from around the corner at the end of the path. Moira ran towards the light, splashing water with every footfall, and turned the corner.

She was blinded by a beam of light that descended from far above her into the chamber. Moira shielded her eyes as she stepped forward. Several tunnels connected here: one ran off ahead of her, another to her right, and still others emptied themselves into the chamber from above her. She stood and waited for her eyes to adjust to the light before she moved forwards, but before Moira could take a step, she froze.

She heard the gurgle, the scrape of claws on rock, the slosh of water. All horribly loud, all horribly close.

In the tunnel across from her, concealed in the faint light, Moira saw the glimmer of slick scales, the hunched frame, the pointed head.

The Terror stepped forwards into the light.

Moira clenched and unclenched her fingers against the hilt of her knife as she stared the creature in the black orbs it had for eyes.

The creature stepped forwards, its mouth held open, waiting for something to pass between its jaws. The siorclan tracked her with its head. The large curved spines lining its back began to twitch as the beast moved closer.

Moira pointed the knife towards the creature as she stepped onto the sandy bank in the middle of the cavern.

The beast surged forwards. Moira hopped back as the jaws snapped at her. She swiped at its head, slicing off a few of the creature's teeth.

The creature thrashed its head towards her, throwing her backwards into the water. The beast leapt on top of her, its claws pressing her into the river bed. With the knife still tight in her grasp, Moira swung it upwards, plunging the blade into the beast's gills.

She burst from the water as she was pulled upwards by the siorclan. She let go of the knife and rolled away from the beast. Her hat was resting on the riverbed while her weapon was stuck in the creature. The beast roared and scraped at the lodged weapon.

Rising to her feet, Moira peeled off her waterlogged coat and readied her blunderbuss. Pointing the bayonet forwards, she charged. The Terror flung the knife into the water and turned to meet Moira's charge.

She leapt at the siorclan, her weapon pointed at its heart. The beast snatched her out of the air and slammed her into the ground. Moira gasped for air in its grasp. The beast pierced her side using its clawed thumb, causing her to cry out.

The Terror roared at her, spraying her face with water. The spray burned her eye. The creature's hand squeezed her. Blind, but with gun still in hand, Moira thrust her bayonet into the creature.

The siorclan bellowed again and threw her. She kept her gun tight in her grip as she landed on the river bank.

Moira crawled to the water and scooped it into her eye. It didn't burn anymore, but her vision was left blurry.

The beast charged towards her. Rolling on her back, Moira pointed the bayonet towards the creature. The blade disappeared into the creature's maw as it snapped its jaws on her gun.

The Terror's teeth dug into the wood of the weapon. Moira cried as pointed teeth pierced her forearm. The creature grabbed her and lifted her off the ground. She punched the beast's eyes with her free hand and used her feet to raise herself higher, stopping it from driving its bottom teeth into her arm. She dug her fingers into its eyes.

It opened its mouth and roared, spilling her onto the ground, teeth protruding from her arm. The Terror stumbled behind her, temporarily blinded. Moira touched her side and winced at the blood that covered her fingers.

She didn't know how long Caspian would take to get there, but she couldn't wait. This thing was going to kill her. Moira pushed herself to her feet just as the siorclan dipped its mouth into the river, scooping water into its chest. It turned back towards her.

Moira ran into the darkness of the tunnel in front of her. The Terror lumbered behind her. She went left, right, straight, then left again.

She sighed as fresh air and daylight beckoned around the next corner, she rushed towards it. A blur of motion caught her eye beside her. Swinging towards it, Moira grasped her gun with both hands and held it lengthways towards her attacker.

The Terror's teeth bit into the weapon. Releasing it, Moira bolted towards the light. Dropping the gun, the beast surged down another path.

Moira turned the corner. At the end of the tunnel, she could see the distant ocean. She rushed towards it. With a roar, the Terror burst into the passage, its shoulder bearing down on her. Drawing another knife, Moira leapt at the beast. She plunged the blade into its shoulder and vaulted over its back.

She rolled to her feet. The beast turned and charged after her, the knife still in its left shoulder.

She ran to the edge of the tunnel and jumped into the waters that raged four storeys below.

CHAPTER 6

P ain ripped through Moira's body as she slammed against the stones. Random quick breaths of air were her only respite between the current's ravaging cycle. Furiously, Moira kicked and pulled herself upwards, trying to grab blindly at anything within reach. She grunted, releasing a stream of bubbles from her mouth when something slammed into her chest, stopping her. Moira gripped it tight and pulled herself to the surface.

She gasped for air when she hauled herself up on top of the boulder. The current continued to pull at her legs, but she stayed firmly anchored. The bandage was torn from her head and her side burned like hell, but she was alive.

Trident Bay was only a short distance away, and the coast was even closer. But they were still too far for her to swim. The current was strong and she was exhausted.

"Hey."

Moira craned her neck.

A pair of hands grabbed her under the arms and hauled her into a small fishing vessel. She stared into the sunburnt face of a man.

"I hope you know how lucky you are! What were you thinking, not wearing a jumper like this?" He pulled at his colourfully dyed jumper. "It's a miracle I saw you."

Moira groaned. "I don't feel that lucky."

"You survived the Terror, that makes you lucky."

"How do you know I fought the Terror?"

She winced as he plucked the tooth out of her arm. She squeezed her hand over the puncture.

He held the tooth up to his face, running a finger over its serrated edge. "The only people crazy enough to go near Lane's Folly are hunters looking to bag the Terror. Well, and me." He turned, brushed half a dozen bottles off of the box beside him, and lifted the lid.

The fisherman pulled out a strip of cloth and passed it to her. "The name's Kevin Corcoran."

"Thank you Kevin." She wrapped the cloth tight around her arm. "I'm Moira."

"So, Moira." He passed her another bandage. "Did you kill it?"

She shook her head as she wound the second bandage around her waist. She could feel the nausea churning in her stomach as the boat rocked to and fro.

Kevin picked up a bottle, pulled out the cork with his teeth, and spat it into the water. "Shame." He drank as he looked out over the water. "Are you going to try again?"

"Yes."

He nodded slowly. He tossed the empty bottle into the water and grabbed the oars. "Let's get you back to shore then."

Moira sat back and closed her eyes as the boat glided forwards.

41

CHAPTER 7

Kevin helped Moira out of the boat. "What's your next move?"

"First I'm going to find Caspian."

He sat back down in his boat. "Caspian?" He spat into the water. "Careful with him, he's not someone I would consider dependable."

She frowned. "I suppose you're right."

"If you're looking for him, he's most likely pinning something of yours to that wall." He used an oar to push himself away from the dock. "If you're looking for help hunting that monster, meet me at my house this evening. Just ask around the old quarter for me. They'll point you in the right direction."

Moira was walked down the dock, still wet, clutching her aching side.

She found Caspian at the memorial, nail in one hand and her hat in the other. Her coat was slung over his left shoulder.

"Stop!"

Caspian looked towards her.

"By the spirits! I can't believe it." He walked towards her with his arms outstretched. "You actually faced the shark-faced bastard and lived!"

Moira snatched her hat from him with one hand and slapped him across the face with the other.

She pulled the hat onto her head as Caspian gave her a cold stare, a small red handprint burning on his cheek.

He smelt of smoke and soil.

"What the hell was that for?"

Moira pointed a finger into his chest. "Where were you?"

"I'm sorry—I tried to get there as fast as I could, but those tunnels are long, and with the Terror stalking them, I couldn't just rush through."

"Did you even look for me?"

Caspian shrugged. "I found your clothes and the blood in the sand. I assumed the worst."

"Give me my coat."

He stood, unmoving.

"What are you waiting for? The coat. Hand it over."

Caspian tossed the garment into her open arms. He winced as he adjusted his suspender with a snap against his skin before looking her up and down. "You look like you've been through hell itself lass. Are you going to be all right?"

"I will be." She sighed, pulling her coat tight around her.

"Oh lass." He grasped her by the shoulders, a smile on his face. "You're exactly what I've been looking for."

CHAPTER 8

"But you look half starved!" Caspian took a seat near the middle of the Windwake's dining hall and beckoned for Moira to sit opposite him. "Come now lass, this is a time for celebration. You're one of the few people to face the Terror and live."

"Shhhh." Moira grabbed his arm. "Just keep this between you and me."

One of Caspian's eyebrow sunk. "But you'll be famous. The people will shout your name, worship the ground you walk on. Don't you want that?"

Moira shook her head. "I don't want anyone to know I'm here. All I want is passage to Qesuis—that's it."

"Well then." Caspian leaned back in his seat, scrutinizing her. "I have to ask. If you're not looking for fame, what is a hunter like you looking for in Qesuis? I thought you might be looking to join those revolutionaries, but you said different." He began to rub his chin. "Then I thought you might be going there to do the opposite. To take the head of that dragon of theirs and the head of his little rider too, but you wouldn't do that if you didn't want fame, so . . ." He leaned forwards again. "Maybe you really are a revolutionary, you're just trying to keep it secret?"

Moira kept her gaze focused on the table. He was asking too many questions. "If I was looking to join the revolution, would you still help me?" she whispered.

Caspian laughed. "As long as you hold up your end of our bargain, I'll hold up mine; but I must say, Shaw will be happy to have a hunter like you in his ranks."

Caspian turned in his seat and scanned his half of the room.

"Can we get some food here? And something to drink?" he called.

Caspian drummed his fingers on the table while Moira kept her hands clasped in front of her.

"Aww, there we are."

A woman scrambled over to their table and presented herself to Caspian, pulling on her white dress and running her hand through her blonde strands.

"I'm really sorry Caspian. I didn't see you come in."

"Really lass, you missed me of all people?"

She grasped his arm and began to sway. "Can you forgive me?"

"Get us something eat and drink quick and I just might."

"What are you having?" the serving girl asked.

"I'll have my usual, which I'm sure you remember." He gave her a wink.

"Yeah, Sleightstone whiskey with fish and potatoes," she answered with a smile.

"Righto lass." Caspian turned his head to look at Moira. "And for you?"

"Anything pork, and just water for me."

"I'll have it out quick as I can." The blonde woman's gaze stayed glued on Caspian.

"That's what I like to hear." Caspian gave her a squeeze around her waist as she turned to leave, eliciting a gleeful squeal from her as she scampered away.

Moira turned up her nose. "Does she always act like that?"

He gave Moira a wink. "Only when I'm here. But I guess it's time we get down to business, isn't it?" Caspian turned in his seat and reached into his pocket. In a flash, he slammed a crimson-smeared knife blade-first into the table, the edge dangerously close to Moira's fingers, causing her to flinch. "I believe this is yours."

She had to wiggle the knife to free it from the wood. The blade came free with a small eruption of splinters, leaving a permanent hole.

"I found it in the water next to your clothes."

"My blunderbuss! Did you find it down there?"

"Sorry lass, only the things I gave back to you."

Moira cursed under her breath and slumped in her chair, leaving the blood-smeared knife lying on the table.

"You'll be needing a new weapon." With a flourish, Caspian tossed his axe into the air and caught it one-handed. "I would recommend getting something like this."

He gave the weapon a few practice chops in the air.

Moira shook her head. "All I need is another gun."

"I don't think another gun is going to help you."

Moira crossed her arms. "And an axe will?"

"An axe like this was made for hunting monsters."

Caspian grasped the head of the weapon and spun it around in his hands, admiring the polished wood handle. "You see lass, you can fire a gun once a minute, and even then you might miss your target."

"I don't just use guns."

"Of course, but all of the weapons you tote around are all about slashing and stabbing and shooting. And firing a gun at a beast is perfectly fine, but a blade, well, that's for fighting a man." He held the axe over the table with both hands, as if to hand it to Moira. "An axe, that's for fighting a beast. When you fight a man you need finesse, quick jabs and cuts when openings appear. When you fight an animal, all you need is brute power." He swung at an invisible enemy beside them. "You see lass? The weight throws the head into your target, helping cause more damage, and it's all focused on this little edge here. Wham!" He slapped his hand against the axe head. "But it's still light enough for someone like you to wield it."

"And what do you mean 'someone like me?'" She raised an eyebrow.

"Someone not as strong as me." Caspian flexed an arm in response.

"I've never used an axe."

"I'll teach you."

"Will that take long?"

Caspian shook his head. "It should only take a few hours to teach you the basics. The rest will need practice."

Moira eyed the weapon. "I'll do it."

Caspian nodded. "We'll start this evening."

The server trotted up and slid her dish-filled tray onto the table, knocking Moira's knife into her lap. Moira sneered at the blonde woman.

"Thanks lass, it smells delicious."

"Thank you." She gave him a smile before slotting her empty tray under her arm. "Are we still meeting tonight?"

"Wouldn't miss it." Caspian gave her a kiss on her hand, letting her leave with a grin on her face.

"Now, back to business." Caspian snatched up his utensils and tore into his fish. He sliced charred bricks complete with breaded seasonings on the pink slab in front of him and shovelled them into his mouth.

"I needed this." He washed his mouthful down with a sip of amber liquid.

Moira cut a piece of meat and left it on her plate. "I was wondering: is Caspian your first name or your last?"

He nodded his head. "Neither and both."

"What do you mean?"

"What I mean is that I only have one name. Caspian. That's it."

"Did you not know your parents, or . . . ?"

"No . . . I had parents, and a name from them, but"—Caspian twisted his mouth—"it didn't . . . I don't know. It—"

"It didn't sound right," Moira interrupted. "Like it was the name of someone else. For someone who didn't exist anymore."

"Yes lass, exactly. It just didn't sound right anymore. That's it."

"So, what happened?"

"Why the sudden interest in me all of a sudden, eh?" He raised an eyebrow as he dropped his fork onto his plate and knitted his fingers in front of his face, elbows on the table.

Moira slotted a sliver of meat into her mouth. "A person doesn't change their name for no reason."

"Ha, too true, too true. Well, I'll regale you with the tale of my life later. We have a busy day ahead of us, and I have meeting tonight, so no more dilly-dallying lass." He used his fork to stab into the stack of meat. Giving her a wink, Caspian pulled his fork back, taking the last of her meal with it.

CHAPTER 9

"So, what is this business of ours exactly?" Moira asked, watching the fury of activity up and down the market street.

"Shopping of course lass."

Moira put a hand on her hip and gave him a suspicious look. "Shopping?"

"Oh yes—well, for me yes. For you"—he pointed to her bandages—"you need to see a doctor. I have a friend that can help. His name is Teague. He's part miracle worker, part mad man, but he hasn't killed anyone. Publicly at least."

"Great, and you're not coming with me?"

"Like I said: shopping. Keep down this road and look for a sign that reads 'Apothecary's End.' After you're done, continue down the street and wait for me near the shop selling the caged beasts."

"Is there anyone else I can go to for help?"

He shrugged. "Sure, but they won't fix you like Teague will. Well, hopefully will." He grinned at her frown. "You'll be fine lass. He's never let me down. Just remember to ask him about the root."

"The root?"

"Yes, the root. And before you go—just hold still for a minute lass." He began sliding his hands down her arms and muttering to himself.

"What are you doing?" Moira cried as he squeezed her ribs.

He slid his hands down to her waist.

"Ow, Caspian?"

He dropped his hands down to her hips.

"Caspian? What are you doing?"

He slid his hands back up her stomach and cupped her breasts. Moira twisted away from his grasp, knocking his hands away as she covered her chest with her arms. "What the fuck was that?"

Caspian tried to touch her shoulders but she pulled away. "Eh now lass, it's a surprise."

"Yes it was, and if you try that again—" Moira brandished her knife and feinted a cut across his groin.

"Woah now, no need for that, just meet me by the cages and you'll be thanking me, I guarantee it."

She strolled down the crowded stall-laden road for several minutes, taking in the colours that surrounded her; the yellows, greens, blues, and reds of brightly painted shops and buildings.

Nestled between the usual bright shops further down stood a drab old building. Moira stopped outside its dark grey exterior. Not a single person passed near its doors or through them.

The sign read *Apothecary's End*.

Moira took a deep breath and ascended to the shop's white door. A red symbol was stained into the grain of the wood—whether it was a ward or a warning, Moira didn't care. She searched for a handle but found none. She pressed her hands against the door, causing it to creak, and a breath of stale air filled with the heat of spice and musk swept past her.

Moira crept into the dim room. It was cluttered with seemingly random collections of books and jars, none of which bore a title or label.

"Why are you here?"

Moira spun to face a robed figure rising from the clutter. The person tilted their head from side to side, their beaked mask sliding first over one eye and then the other.

Moira pulled her coat back, revealing the bloodied bandage. "I need help."

"There are many places you could find help." The figure pointed to the ground. "But why are you here?"

"I was told to find Teague."

"By whom?"

"Caspian."

"Hmmm, Caspian, really? Did he ask for something specific?" The man stroked the bottom of the beak with his knuckles.

"He told me to ask about a root."

"That's all I needed to hear. Wait a moment."

The figure pulled books from the wall and flung them over his shoulder. He then pulled a panel from the bookshelf. Tapping his mask's beak, the figure eyed the hidden collection.

"I am the one known as Teague, if you havn't already guessed." He continued tapping out a rhythmic pattern, bobbing his head to the beat.

"Wait." Teague stood erect and rushed to a collection of stacked bowls. "Here we are." He held one of the bowl with both hands. "Just a bit of moisture and it should be fine. This might burn a bit, but from the look of those scars that shouldn't be a problem."

He scraped the sides of the bowl with his gloved fingers. After gathering the crimson dust at the bottom of the bowl, he held it up to her face.

"Spit."

Moira spat into the bowl, and Teague began mixing the two together. It smelt of smoke and soil.

"What is that?"

"The root." He scraped the paste out of the bowl. "Hold still."

He tore the bandage off of her arm and smeared the mixture across the bite marks. He twisted his head back and forth.

"There seems to be an infection setting in." Teague scooped up a glob of paste and spread it across her side.

Moira hissed as he poked a finger into her wound.

"We won't have to worry about that for much longer." He took a step back.

Warmth spread through her skin.

"How does it feel?"

"Warm."

"Hmm, any pain?"

"No."

"Just wait."

Moira could almost hear the smile in his tunnelled voice. She twitched as the heat began to sting her flesh.

"Aww, just wait," the beaked apothecary said as he leaned next to his stack of bowls.

The heat continued to build, the scent growing more pungent as well. Moira began to sweat, her breath laboured.

"This root is rare, even in its home nation far, far to the east."

It began to burn.

"It took a tremendous amount of time and money to bring this root here, but its properties are amazing."

Moira glanced down at her wounds. Her skin began to hiss. Yanking a glove off, she shoved it into her mouth and bit down.

"In the easterners' native tongue it is known as Xi Han, but I like to refer to it as devil's bargain. You get what you want, but you'll burn for it."

She clutched her hands into fists and stood, shaking.

"Not much longer."

A puff of smoke and fire flashed in the crevasses of Moira's wounds, causing an explosion of pain. Moira screamed through her glove.

The heat faded.

Teague jumped and clapped. "That never gets old. Go, go ahead. Look at it!"

Moira let the glove drop from her mouth and breathed slowly. She glided her bare hand over the injuries.

The wound had shrunk down to a small divot, and the skin around it was completely healed.

"How is that possible?!" She slid her hand over it. A sharp sting pierced her side as she touched the divot, causing her to hiss through her teeth.

"Careful there. It's miraculous, not perfect."

"How much for it?" Moira asked.

"Caspian sent you, Caspian pays."

"How much for more?"

"I have none for sale; all of it is Caspian's. You're lucky

you got what little you did," Teague said as he returned to his clutter. "Now, I must get back to my own business."

Moira thanked him as she retrieved her glove. Teague bowed in response as she burst back out into the market. The meeting spot Caspian had described was not far.

Stacked upon each other were multiple cages, many of which housed creatures. All but one contained a hound of one breed or another. In one cage lay a barghest, native to Abalon. The goblin-wolf rested its olive-skin head on its equally bare legs.

Moira watched the creature calmly breathe in and out of its pointed, narrow snout as she waited. She wondered if Lincoln had ever encountered one.

Caspian walked up beside her. "Are you looking for a pet lass?"

"No, that one just reminds of someone I know."

"Surely they're not that ugly?"

"Forget it. What is all of this?"

Caspian thrust a box towards her. "Open it."

He held the box as Moira pulled the top off. Inside were an assortment of brown leathers and cream-coloured clothes.

"Clothes?"

"The newest fashions from Qesuis. I figured you might need something to blend in there. I tried to get your size right." He flexed his fingers in a groping motion. "I usually get the size right, so hopefully they fit."

"Why are . . ."

"Wait a second lass," Caspian said, handing the box to Moira. He then pulled an eyepatch out of his pocket. "This is yours." He held it up to her face. "I had them attach the two ends with a clasp. Here." He looped it over her head and closed the clasp. The patch held tight against her face.

"And here." He opened the clasp, letting the patch fall into his hand. He then put it back on her, carefully adjusting it to rest comfortably on her face. "Okay lass, what did you want to say?"

Moira could feel the heat in her cheeks. "I don't understand. Why are you giving me all of this?"

He gave her a wink. "Can't have the hero of Trident Bay looking like she gets her clothes from corpses, can we? Anyways lass, let's see if those clothes fit."

CHAPTER 10

C aspian led the way to a set of gates.

The guard on duty sprung awake at the sound of their approach and pulled the wrought iron door open.

Caspian strode through, Moira close behind. The soft clack of their heels was the only sound as they strolled between the well-manicured bushes separating them from the estates that lay beyond. Carved stone creatures standing sentinel in the gardens tracked their progress with unwavering stares.

"This one."

Caspian steered her towards an estate to their left. The building shone. Its yellow exterior shamed the subtle greys and whites of its neighbours.

"Welcome to my home."

Caspian pushed the door open and led her through.

"Where the hell have you been?" A powder-faced man stormed up to them, thrusting a finger at Moira as he leered up at Caspian. "Who the fuck is this?"

Moira swung away from the gathering nobles that sat around the table before them.

Caspian grabbed her by the shoulders and whispered into her ear. "Whoa now, its okay lass. Go upstairs, this won't take long. Choose any room you like."

Moira nodded and shielded her face with her package as she took off to find the stairs.

"We've been waiting for two hours now Caspian, waiting to hear your plans for this week, and what were you doing? Running around with some whore again?"

"Only two hours Gaspard? I was aiming for three."

Moira stopped on the stairs, hearing Gaspard's wailing.

"The old quarter is being whipped into a frenzy. I fled Qesuis to avoid an uprising, and now there're mobs forming just streets away from my home, and you seem content to ignore it. For the love of Antoine, why did I listen to a scale-eating, dirty-nailed scratcher like you?"

Moira paused as she heard the what sounded like a crack of thunder.

"Do you think I haven't been doing anything? Plunkett is trying to rally them against me and unless one of you knows where he's hiding, we're reliant on Captain Toal, who I've tasked with capturing him. If any of you have a better plan, I would love to hear it!"

Silence.

"None of you? Not even you Gaspard?"

Silence.

"Fine then. Now, on to other business. The curse of the Terror has kept true for Kavanagh and his sons. Patrick's widow is willing to sell. O'Sullivan, what else is on the . . ."

Moira finished her ascent as their conversation turned to mundane city planning. She peered into the countless rooms lining the hall. Many were littered with antiquities, pieces of art, furniture, old weapons—and all of them were covered in layers of dust.

Moira chose a room located at the back of the house. A lone ray of sun warmed the bed, which sat in the middle of the room. She lowered the box to the floor and closed the door behind her. Throwing her hat onto the bed, Moira pulled the blinds closed and let her coat drop, kicking up a small cloud of dust. She unbuckled her holsters and dropped them at the foot of the bed with her scarf.

She crouched down to the box, flipped open the lid, and pulled out her new clothes.

She stripped off her old scavenged clothes and tossed them into the corner near the door. She slipped on her new blouse, trousers, and boots.

A knock came at the door.

"Come in."

"Perfect lass!" Caspian clapped his hands. "Just perfect. Am I the best or what?"

"The neckline is lower then I'm used to." Moira pulled up on the fabric.

Caspian closed the gap between them. "It looks good."

He pulled one of her hands away. Using his finger, he traced the scar that slashed across her chest. Starting at her collar, he travelled down, caressing the soft skin of her breast.

Moira pulled away and grabbed her coat. "Is your meeting done?" she asked, brushing the faint trace of white powder from her chest.

"It won't be done for a while. I just took a bit of a break to check up on you."

"What happened to Gaspard?" She closed up her coat.

"Gaspard? Oh, he's all right lass. He just gets a little worked up and needs some help calming down. He's been through a lot."

"Will there be enough time to train?" Moira replaced her hat.

Caspian pulled an axe out from behind him and tossed it towards her in one fluid motion. Moira caught it with both hands and inspected the worn and pitted weapon.

"Don't worry, I'll make the time. I have a nice little place in mind, somewhere we can be alone."

"How long until we leave?"

Caspian rubbed his chin. "Five, six hours."

"Great, I'll meet you here." Moira grabbed her hat.

Caspian grabbed her arm. "Whoa now, are you headed somewhere?"

"Kevin Corcoran asked me to meet him this evening."

He released her arm. "The fisherman?"

"He fished me out of the ocean after I escaped from the Terror. He's going to help me hunt the Terror."

Caspian crossed his arms. "Go, speak with him, but tell me everything the codger tells you."

CHAPTER 11

Moira stood at the border of the city's old quarter. A line of guards stood behind a fence, listening as a chant rang through the quarter. Voices shouting: "Spread the wealth," "Opportunity for all," and "Down with the tyrant!"

"I'm captain Liam Toal." A guardsman strode up to her, one hand outstretched, the other gripping a handle of a club. The weapon's bulbous head rested on his shoulder. "Why do you want to go through the barrier?"

Moira shook his hand. "I have business in the old quarter."

The captain slipped a bean into his mouth and crushed it between his teeth. He spoke through the corner of his mouth. "And what business would that be?"

"I need to speak with Kevin Corcoran."

The captain nodded his head. "Things are going to turn violent soon, but if you don't mind being caught up in that, I'll let you through." He patted his weapon. "Once rein-forcements get here, I'm ending this rally."

She nodded.

The captain slipped another bean into his mouth, crunching it between his teeth.

He turned towards the guards. "All right boys, let this one through."

The guardsmen grabbed the fence and pulled them apart. Once Moira was through, they dropped the barrier back into place.

She turned to the captain. "Do you know the way to Corcoran's home?"

Toal leaned against the fence. "Move through the court-yard. Two blocks down this road, turn right. His shack is the fourth on the left. Be quick about it."

A crowd of a few hundred formed in a courtyard past the barrier.

A man, his once-fine clothes now dirty and torn, stood on a roof above the gathering. He waved his hands up and down, bidding the crowd to chant louder.

She moved along the edges of the courtyard, far from the edge of the crowd.

Moira's boots squished in the mud as she followed the Captain's directions. A group of men stood watching her progress. She spotted the shimmer of sharpened metal underneath their folded arms.

Walking with her gaze held forwards, Moira brushed her coat aside with her hand. The gang's gaze left her as they spotted her arsenal.

The fisherman's home was a shack squeezed between two homes twice its size. Faded red paint flaked off of its wooden door when Moira knocked.

Kevin pulled the door open. "In here."

The fisherman closed the door behind her and barred it with a wooden board. He then hurried to pull out a chair for her at his table. "Did Caspian buy you those clothes?"

"He did," she said as she sat down.

Kevin took the seat across from her. A bottle was in his hand. "What does he want from you?"

"He wants me to help him kill the Terror of Trident Bay."

Kevin leaned back in his chair, his forehead crinkled. "Typical." He yanked the cork out with his mouth.

"Typical?"

The fisherman nodded. "The man's a bloody coward. He knows about the curse of the Terror, but does he do anything about it?" He shook his head. "No, but he's more than happy to gloat about how he fought the beast."

Moira held her palms out to him. "Slow down Kevin. What's this curse you're talking about?"

He sighed and used his free hand to rub his eyes. "The curse of the Terror. I recognized a pattern in the creature's attacks." He took a swig. "The creature goes after smaller coastal vessels. There's a ship leaving tomorrow that's a prime target for the bastard."

Moira leaned forwards. "What's the name of the ship?"

"*The Fortune's Tide*. She was recently acquired by Alistair Sand, a man I happen to know personally." He took a drink. "I've told him about you. He's hoping you'll join his voyage."

"How long is the trip?"

"Two days."

Moira frowned. The next full moon was in two days, but she would make it work; she had too. "I'll be there."

He grinned. "We'll meet you tomorrow morning by the monument." He rose from his chair and beckoned her to the door. "You should leave; the guards will be breaking up the protest soon."

A single voice raged through the old quarter. "Caspian

has cheated you, forced you to live in filth. He speaks of prosperity but has left you with nothing. He fences you in like cattle."

Captain Liam Toal led a column of a dozen guards through the streets as Moira approached the courtyard. The captain bounced his club in his hand. "All right everyone, time to clear out." He pointed to the man on the roof. "Except you, Plunkett. You stay."

"Caspian promises safety yet sends his goon to beat you into submission." Plunkett raised his fist to the air. "We will bring down the tyrant."

Toal rested the club on his shoulder. "They only have to worry if they plan on resisting." He walked towards the crowd. "And I said to clear out."

A member of the crowd surged towards the captain, a dagger in his hand. Toal swung his weapon, catching his attacker in the head, causing the man to drop to the ground, his body limp. "Boys, clear them out."

The guards raised their guns and fired above the crowd.

Moira pressed herself against the side of the street as hundreds fled the guards. Plunkett fled as well, jumping off the back of the building.

A few dozen members of the crowd, armed with daggers and clubs, charged the guards.

Gripping their rifles like clubs, the guards rushed to meet them. Outnumbered three to one, several guards fell under the crush of their attackers.

Moira rushed forwards to aid the captain and his men. Pulling out her axe, she swung the blunt side of the weapon into one of the mob member's head, dropping the man to the ground.

Snatching up the man's fallen club, Moira swung at the next member of the mob. He too fell to the ground.

A guard near her cried out in pain and disappeared behind his three attackers. Raising bloodied weapons with a cheer, the aggressors searched for their next victim.

They spotted Moira with two of their comrades at her feet. With a yell they ran towards her, weapons at the ready.

Moira dropped the club and drew her pistols, but the rebels came on unfazed.

She pulled the triggers.

Two of them dropped, clutching their sides. The third, a woman, slashed with her dagger.

Moira flipped her grip on the pistols and blocked the blade with the butt of one pistol. With the other, she struck the woman in the face.

The woman dropped the blade and clutched her bloodied face. Moira struck the woman again, driving her attacker to her knees. With a final strike, the woman fell to the ground.

The last of the mob ran as the guards gained the upper hand.

"Thanks for the assistance." Toal strode over to Moira. He passed a member of the mob on his hands and knees. The captain gave him a kick, dropping him.

Moira pointed over to a row of three dead guards. "I'm sorry about your men."

Toal bashed his club into the gunshot wound of one of the murderers, causing him to cry out. "These fuckers are going to pay for it, I promise you that." He gave Moira a pat on shoulder and pointed to the fence. "Best if you get out of here."

She nodded and left to meet Caspian.

CHAPTER 12

Moira wrapped her arms around her waist in an attempt to seal out the cold evening breeze.

She and Caspian stood in the ruins of a long-abandoned tower far from the city limits. Only a single section of brick wall remained standing, defiantly resisting the strangling roots of a nearby tree.

Caspian paced the circular limits of their arena, spinning his axe again and again with every stride. His second blade—a sword—rested against his covered shoulder.

"The difference between using a blade and an axe is simple." He held his weapon ready.

"With a blade, you make thrusts, you slash at your enemy. Then you raise your guard before an enemy can strike back." He mirrored the motions with his sword.

"With an axe, you can't chop at your enemy. That leaves you vulnerable, it tires you out. No; axes are all about momentum."

He set the weapon in motion, cutting arcs in front of him, letting gravity pull the axe down before twisting and swinging down in the other direction.

Caspian approached a small piece of firewood with his sword at the ready. With a flick of his wrist, the slender blade slashed across the wood, shaving off a thin sliver of bark.

"Not much, right?" He slashed another sliver of bark off the wood. "Now watch this."

He plunged the blade into the ground beside him and grasped the axe in both hands. Raising it above his head he brought it down in a powerful stroke. The head of the axe buried itself deep within the wood, splitting it down the centre. Caspian lifted the weapon and the wood came with it before falling back to the ground.

He turned to Moira with a raised eyebrow.

Moira gave him a slow clap. "You chopped wood with an axe. Congratulations." She lifted her axe and mimicked Caspian's motions. "Look, this isn't difficult."

Caspian smiled.

"What? Seriously, why bring me all the way out here for this?"

"Hit that tree." He pointed to the tree strangling what was left of the tower.

"Fine." She began walking towards it.

"No, from where you are."

Moira paused and squinted her eye at him.

"Throw it."

She planted her feet, lifted the weapon over her shoulder, and hurled it. She was rewarded with the ring of metal on stone and Caspian's laughter.

"Like this."

He flung his axe forwards. The weapon severed a limb off of the tree before sticking into its trunk.

"All right, okay. I admit that would come in handy."

Caspian wrenched his axe out of the tree and fished hers out of the fallen leaves.

He slid his axe into his belt and moved up behind her. "Your stance is terrible."

He placed his hands on her: one on her hip the other on her shoulder. He slid them down as he spoke in her ear. "Slow now, feel the weight of it. Don't tense up—keep your body relaxed. Those clothes were made to let your body move, so move! Loosen your grip—not that much—yes, just like that. You'll tire yourself out holding it that tight. And then back over, careful, that's it. You feel that? How it carries through with the swing? Then through the recovery, back into the swing again. You're a natural, lass."

Caspian broke away, letting Moira continue the movements without him.

"Now strike!"

Moira pushed all of her strength into her swing. The head of the weapon bit into the bark, spitting splinter into the air around it.

"A good hit! Excellent lass, you even put your weight into it. That's good, very good. Here, let me show you some more."

He snatched his axe from his belt. "Try moving your grip up and down the shaft. All right, now try giving it a few swings. What do you feel?"

She let the shaft slide through her fingers after every stroke. "It doesn't feel as heavy and I have a bit more control over how it moves."

"Exactly lass, exactly. Now let it slide all the way down."

Moira let the shaft fall until the head hit the top of her hand, the blade hanging in front of her fingers. She punched forwards, using the axe head as bladed knuckles.

"You're right handed?"

"Yes."

"Then stand with your right foot forwards." He pulled her leg forwards. "Hold it with both hands and keep it behind your back."

Moira grasped the shaft of the axe with both hands and held the weapon in front of her with her arms outstretched. She bent her arms, moving the weapon over her head, and held it parallel with her back, her arms bent over her shoulders.

"Okay, now, when you throw, don't throw too hard or too early." Caspian stood beside her and mirrored her stance. "Like this."

He brought both of his hands over his head in a chopping motion, rotating his shoulders in a smooth motion, stopping with his arms extended. "Don't flick your wrists. Now, you try."

Moira mirrored his chopping motion, brought the axe over her head, and released it, her arms extended. The weapon flew through the air before bouncing off the ground.

"Better lass, but you flicked your wrists."

Moira let out a slow breath before retrieving the axe. "I don't know what you mean."

He held his hands out in front of him, his wrists aligned with his arms. "When it gets to this part just let it go, don't try to give it extra force with your wrists. Just keep them like this." He bent his wrists down. "Not like this."

Moira took another breath and got back into position. She threw the weapon again, releasing it with her wrists straight. The weapon flew through the air and buried itself into the trunk of the tree.

She jumped and cheered and hurried to retrieve her weapon.

"There you go lass, well done, very well done."

Moira stood waving the axe between her fingers. "Just a few more throws like that, and the Terror won't stand a chance."

"Whoa there, that's basically all you need to know." Caspian glanced at the darkening sky before sitting on a boulder. "Just keep practicing."

Moira struck her throwing pose and tossed the axe again.

"Now that the lesson is over, what did the fisherman tell you?" Caspian said, tapping a finger against the stone.

"He believes that the Terror will attack a ship and I've volunteered to protect the vessel."

Caspian leaned forward. "Which vessel?"

Moira yanked the weapon free. *"The Fortune's Tide.* The captain goes by the name of Alistair Sand."

"Sand eh?" He stared forwards, rubbing his chin.

Moira stood in front of him, axe resting on her shoulder. "Are you coming along for the voyage?"

"How long is the trip?"

"Thirty-six hours."

Caspian turned away. "Sorry lass, I can't afford to be away for that long."

She stepped towards him. "I know it may not be a sure thing, but if Kevin is right, it's worth the time. . ."

"Did he say anything else?"

Moira crossed her arms. "He said you were a coward."

Caspian rose from the boulder and turned to her, fists clenched. "A coward?" He pulled the neck of his sweater, revealing the scars that cut across his chest. "I got these scars fighting the motherfucker—do you know what scars the fisherman has? None. I need to stay here; the situation in the old quarter is getting worse, Moira, that's what's really worth my time."

She frowned. "I know how bad it's gotten. I was there today. Toal lost three men."

Caspian closed his eyes and let out a breath. "The beast needs to be dealt with, but all of this shite is taking up too much of my time. That's why I recruited you. Take the voyage, kill the Terror."

Caspian slipped a key out of his vest pocket and passed it to her.

"Sleep in my house tonight. Use any bedroom you like, except the one with the gold posts—that one is mine. Unless you want to share it." He forced a smile and gave her a wink. "Other than that, do as you please. We're partners now lass. Together we're going to make Trident Bay safe."

Moira couldn't sleep. It wasn't the giggles or cries coming from Caspian's bedroom that kept her awake. She stared at the moon. It was three quarters full and filling.

CHAPTER 13

M oira spent the morning in the backyard of Caspian's estate. Surrounded by the abundance of green that clung to the boundaries of the space, she practiced with her axe, sweeping and chopping at the invisible scaled horrors that bared down on her.

"Nice movement, very natural. The axe is a good fit for you."

Caspian leaned against the doorway.

She let the weapon come to a rest by her leg and stood, taking in a few slow breaths.

"Have you come up with a solution for Plunkett yet?"

He stepped out of the doorway and approached her. "I'm still coming up with something. Do you want breakfast?"

Moira shook her head. "I need to meet with the crew this morning."

"Are you sure lass? Will they be feeding you during the trip?"

"I don't know."

"Well then," He slipped his arm behind her back,

turning her towards the house. "Let's have something to eat. I had my cook come in specially for you."

He led her past the large conference table to a small table set up near the kitchen. A steady wave of scents wavered towards them—Moira could pick out cooked meats, butter, and bread. Caspian pulled out a rickety little chair before settling into his own, emitting a series of creaks and cracks with every movement. He sat sideways in his chair, preventing their knees colliding underneath the table.

"Did I ever tell you how I achieved all of this?"

"No, you were going to though."

"Ah! Then you're in for a treat. You've been through the old quarter, right?"

She nodded. "Yesterday during the rally."

"Yes of course, forgive me. Anyway, five years ago that's what all of Trident Bay looked like. There were no bustling streets, no booming trade, nothing. Then two things happened. I was a labourer on a ship called *The Ranalt*. We were running a job for one of the dozen trading companies that operated out of Trident Bay at the time. The Twin Leaf company I think? It's not that important. Anyway, our ship was raided by fucking pirates. There had to be a hundred of the bloody bastards! I slew a dozen of them single-handedly, but they took the ship. I was the only one who survived their raid and only because I was pushed overboard and left to die in the ocean. I was rescued by a merrow while I was—"

Moira kicked the table. "A merrow rescued you? Really? Was it a mermaid or a merman?"

Caspian laughed. "Ha, yes it's true, and it was a mermaid, I'll never forget the sight of her. Oh, she was a beauty. I don't know how something so dainty dragged me onto that coast, but I'll never forget how her skin shimmered in the sunlight . . ." He stared into space for a few moments before shaking his head clear.

"Anyways lass, back to the story! I was picked up by a passing ship soon after. That was the first thing. Now, the second thing that happened was the rise of the Terror. Whatever pitiful trade we had here before, the Terror obliterated it. Almost all of the companies wanted out. They lost ships, men—even some of the owners themselves fell victim to the creature." He leaned forwards with a grin on his face. "Where everyone else saw ruin, I saw opportunity. Using a bit of coin I had saved up over the years, I bought out the Trident Bay Trading Company."

"You bought an entire company with your savings?"

"Like I said lass, things were bad. They lost four ships in the span of a week, one of which carried the owner of the company. They had just two ships left in their fleet. It wasn't long before I bought the others out too."

"And your ships weren't attacked."

"In the beginning they were, but not so much anymore."

"Why?"

"When I heard about the attacks on my ships and about where the beast lived, I decided to do something about it. I travelled to Lane's Folly and fought the beast. It left the ships alone for a while and now our ships are too large for the beast to target—there're too many people on board. It preferred the smaller boats, like the one you're taking."

Moira gave him a nod. "So, you built a single trading company out of a dozen others so you could compete with the larger traders."

"Exactly lass, but that's not the only opportunity I took advantage of. There were a number of Qesuis nobles with enough sense to flee the revolution. I gave them a place where they could move their fortunes while continuing to live their luxury lifestyles."

"Like Gaspard."

"Yes, like our dear friend Gaspard. Not all of the nobles who fled survived the trip, so their fortunes ended up funding the growth of the city." He clapped his hands. "Breakfast is here."

A woman in an apron placed two plates in front of them, each heaped with food.

"Impressive," Moira said, pulling a strip of bacon out from under the buttered bread and eggs that buried it.

"And it's only getting better. Since that dragon joined the revolution last year, nobles have been begging for sanctuary here."

The cook returned, placing glasses for them and filling them with an amber liquid.

Caspian grabbed his and lifted it towards Moira. "To opportunities, and those who take advantage of them."

Moira returned the gesture, banging her glass against his, but didn't drink.

CHAPTER 14

M oira found the fisherman staring at the collection nailed to the memorial board, his hands held behind his back.

"Hard to believe that one beast could cause so much death." Kevin turned to her. "So much pain."

Moira stood beside him. "They'll get their justice soon."

"True enough." He patted her shoulder. "I'm glad to see you—there're not many people who would willingly face such a beast."

"Are you coming along?"

He shook his head. "I'm an old fisherman, what good will I be to you? I've seen the Terror once, and that's enough for me."

"You've seen the Terror?"

"I had a shipping company of my own before the beast appeared. My ship was the first he targeted." Kevin stepped towards the memorial and tapped a half-dozen scraps of sun-bleached fabric. "These belonged to my crew."

"I'm sorry."

He sighed. "It's all right—I may have had to sell my

business, but I make a better living than most." He gave Moira a weak smile. "Anyway, I'm going to get my justice soon enough."

Moira nodded. "I promise you: I'll kill the beast."

"I know you will."

A thin man approached the pair. His auburn hair was tousled and most of his clothes were dirty, but he wore a fresh black captain's coat and bicorne. He smiled at them with what few teeth he had.

"Moira, may I introduce Captain Alistair Sand."

Alistair tipped his hat to her. "I'm so happy you agreed to come. My crew and I feel a lot safer with you aboard."

Kevin slapped Alistair's shoulder. "How are preparations coming along with the ship?"

"We're ready to leave whenever Moira is ready."

She nodded. "Lead the way."

Moira hung over the edge of the ship clutching her stomach. The water churned against the hull and her guts churned with it. With a final retch, she flipped to rest her elbows against the railing.

Only three of Captain Sand's crew were present on the deck. They milled about, hands tightly gripping the handles of their weapons as they peered through the dark.

Moira closed her eye and yawned as she slid down to sit on the deck. She focused on her breathing while listening to the creak of wood and the click of shoes.

The ship lurched behind her, forcing her back.

She opened her eye and saw webbed claws gripping the railing several paces in front.

"It's here!" she shouted.

The ship steadied itself as the Terror hauled itself

aboard, tossing her forwards before slamming her back into the railing.

She rubbed the back of her head with one hand and snatched her axe with the other. The crew cursed and stumbled across the deck.

The Terror surged towards the crew member in front of it, a broad shouldered middle-aged man. The crew member slashed with his sword, cutting across the creature's chest. The Terror slammed into him, grasping him in its claws.

Moira pulled out her pistols and fired into the beast's back.

The creature roared as the man squirmed and cried in the creature's grasp. The Terror snapped its jaws down onto the man's shoulder. Dropping his weapon, he screamed and clawed at his attacker.

With a vicious thrash of the Terror's head, the man went limp. Tearing and swallowing a chunk of flesh from the man's body, the beast dropped the severed hand and tossed what was left of the man's torso onto the deck.

Moira gripped her axe with both hands and held her ground. Another man, this one tall and wiry, stood beside her. The last crewman, a stout bald man, retreated into the lower deck.

The Terror charged towards her, ribbons of flesh draped between its teeth.

Moira dashed to her right, putting the ship's mast between her and the beast. Her ally did the same.

The beast left gouges in the ship's mast as it swung around it with its webbed claws. It lunged towards her.

Moira threw herself to the right while her ally threw himself to the left.

The beast crashed onto the deck between them, rocking the boat.

Moira grabbed the railing as a wave of nausea gripped her. The Terror pushed itself to its feet as it lumbered towards her, jaws snapping. She raised the axe above her head and buried it in the creatures pointed snout.

The weapon stuck fast and the creature thrashed its head, breaking her grip on the weapon and tossing her against the railing of the ship.

Her ally thrust his sword into the beast's back.

The Terror knocked him to the deck with a swing of its arm. As the beast turned back to Moira, she gripped her axe and yanked it free.

The creature threw its head up, flipping her over the railing.

Moira plunged into the water.

Bursting through the surface with a gasp, she grabbed her tricorn which floated beside her and slammed it back on her head. She chopped her axe into the hull of the ship and used it to pull herself out of the water. Gripping the railing, she hauled herself back onto the ship.

The Terror snatched up the fallen crewman from the deck, its claws digging into the man's thigh and head. Lifting the man into its mouth, the beast tore out his stomach with a thrash of its head.

The doors to the lower deck exploded outward.

Captain Sand charged through the doorway with his last four crewmen. The stout crewman stepped forwards, pointing a blunderbuss towards the creature.

The Terror dropped its victim and with a retch of its gut sprayed the group with blood-tinged water and chunks of flesh.

Only the stout man shielded his eyes from the torrent. The rest screamed and clawed at their eyes as the beast approached them. The stout man pointed the weapon towards the creature and pulled the trigger.

Nothing happened.

He dropped the weapon and stumbled backwards.

"Over here," Moira called.

The Terror kept its eyes locked on the captain.

Moira placed her foot forward, lifted the axe over her head, and hurled it.

The weapon spun through the air before slamming into the Terror's back.

The creature arched its back and roared.

Moira charged the beast with her knife drawn.

The Terror shook with rage as it turned towards her. It swiped at her, but Moira dodged with a quick side step. A second slash cut into her back and threw her to the deck. She rolled onto her back and readied her knife.

The beast slammed its left hand down on top of her. Moira had the wind knocked out of her as she drove the blade through the creature's hand. The Terror pushed down on her. She struggled for breath. With a groan of effort, Moira tore the blade up through the creature's hand, splitting the webbing between its claws. She held the freed blade over her head and drove it into the creature's wrist.

Her vision began to fade.

Pulling the blade free, she drove it back in.

The Terror shook and roared.

Gripping the knife with both hands, Moira tore the blade sideways, cutting a path through the creature's arm.

The creature pulled its hand off of her and retreated, holding its injured hand against its chest.

Captain Sand clutched at his eyes with one hand and slashed at the creature's back.

Moira coughed and sucked in air as her vision returned.

Rising to her feet, she reversed her grip on her knife and came at the beast again.

The Terror turned its attention to the captain. Using its right hand, it grabbed him by the shoulder.

Moira plunged the knife into the creature's back next to her axe and pulled both weapons free.

The captain swung at the Terror with his free arm. The beast shook as it caught the captain's left forearm between its jaws and tore it from his body.

Alistair fell to the ground screaming as he clutched the ragged stump.

The Terror spun around, knocking Moira's weapons out of her hands, and flung her to the ground.

The beast bore down on her as she grabbed the forgotten blunderbuss and swung it as like a club at the creature's head. The butt of the weapon collided with the Terror's jaws, spraying a dozen teeth across the deck.

The Terror snapped at her.

Moira knocked its head back with another swing, knocking free more teeth.

A woman, her eyes red, drove a spear into the creature's side.

The Terror pulled the weapon from her grasp. As she tried to retreat, the creature lunged at her, snapping its jaws around her side.

The woman screamed as she was dragged to the ground. With a thrash of the beast's head, she went limp.

Moira rose to a crouch and wiped the flint of the weapon dry with her sleeve. She pointed the weapon and pulled the trigger.

Nothing.

The Terror dropped the corpse of the woman and turned towards Moira. It charged.

Moira blew on the flint, pulled back the hammer, and pulled the trigger.

The flash blinded her.

Rounds tore through the Terror's side, shredding the flesh. Moira rolled out of the way of the creature as it crashed into the railing and fell into the water, leaving a trail of blood behind it.

Moira blinked her vision clear and tossed the weapon to the ground. She retrieved her axe before peering over the edge of the ship.

The Terror was nowhere to be seen.

She let out a long slow breath before rushing to the captain.

Alistair was pale. A belt and piece of rope were tied around his bicep, and a blood-soaked cloth was wrapped around his elbow. "Did you kill it?" He shook as he leaned against the doors to the lower deck.

Moira placed her hand on his shoulder and nodded. "I killed it."

Alistair smiled before passing out.

Moira turned to the remaining crew. "Take us to the nearest port."

CHAPTER 15

I t took two hours to reach their destination.

A guardsman yawned as he waved to them from the dock. "Welcome to Calden, prepare for board . . ." His eyes widened as they pulled in next to him.

The corpses were absent from the deck of the ship, but the blood was still smeared across the wood planks.

Alistair was carried off the ship by Moira and one of his crew, while the others stayed to finish docking the ship and explaining the situation to the guard.

Moira's stomach dropped as she glimpsed an illustration of her face amongst the dozens of other wanted posters lining the walls of the guard's post. She shielded her face against Alistair as she carried him into town.

With only two dozen small wooden houses, a healer was easy to find.

Moira and the crewman laid Alistair on the bed before retreating to a small waiting area while the healer, an elderly woman, hunched over him.

Moira sat in the corner of the room, cloaking her face in

the shadows. The crewman, a younger tanned man, took the seat next to her.

They sat in silence for half an hour.

The healer shuffled into the room. Her fingers were stained red.

The crewman rose from his seat. "Is he all right?"

She tapped his arm. "He needs some food and just a little time."

Moira spoke. "How much time?"

"Two or three days. Unless infection sets in—then I don't know."

Moira cursed under her breath.

The crewman stepped forwards. "Can I see him?"

The elderly woman nodded and stepped aside, letting the man rush into the next room.

Moira rose from her chair and leaned towards the healer.

"What's the fastest way to Trident Bay?" She whispered.

"You aren't waiting for your friend?"

She shook her head. "I have urgent business."

"Right then, right then. Sorry to tell you, but the fastest way would be walking."

"Walking?"

"The ferry won't travel there anymore, and the carriage won't be back for another two days."

Moira sighed. "How long?"

The healer hummed and tapped her chin. "Day and a half, less if you're fast."

Moira thanked the older woman and pulled her scarf over her face before slipping out the door.

She kept her head down as she followed the line of

erected logs that served as the town's wall. She jumped into a gap between two houses as she heard guards approaching.

The guardsmen arrows clanged together in the quivers at their belts as they marched past her. Gravel crunched under their boots.

She slipped out of her hiding place and followed the wall.

Her path ended at the gates.

They were closed and were guarded by a woman. Her dark hair was tied into a braid that rested over her shoulder. A collection of wanted posters were plastered on the gates.

"Hey you," the guardswoman called to her, waving Moira forwards. "Come here." The guardswoman twisted the string of her bow with her fingers. "I've never seen you here before."

Moira pulled her scarf down. "A boat brought me in a few hours ago."

"What brings you to Calden?"

"I was supposed to go to further down the coast." Moira clutched her stomach. "But I was getting horribly seasick, so they let me off here."

"You thinking of staying awhile?"

Moira pointed to the gate. "Actually, I'm looking to leave."

The guardswoman jumped to attention. "Oh, sorry about that. Here, allow me." She slipped her bow over her shoulder and approached the gate with Moira. "We don't get many visitors here."

The guardswoman grabbed the gate door and pulled it open. "There you are."

Moira nodded and walked through the doorway.

"Hold a minute." The guardswoman grabbed her shoulder.

Moira spun around.

The guardswoman studied the posters. "This one kind of looks..."

Moira's fist smashed into the other woman's nose. The guard stumbled back holding her nose. Moira followed up with a punch to the guardswoman's stomach, doubling her over. "Sorry." Moira said as she kicked her in the chest.

The guardswoman fell onto her back and wailed as Moira bolted through the gate and down the road.

Night descended upon Moira.

She found a large thicket to conceal her; it wasn't ideal, but it was the best she could do.

Moira packed her clothes and gear into a neat package before hiding them amongst the twisted branches of the trees behind her, shielding them from the downpour that soaked the soil.

On her knees wrapped in her coat, she closed her eye, shivering from the cold and from the onslaught of pain that tore at her mind.

Sparse rays of moonlight broke through the mass of clouds, casting shadows around her before fading away a moment later.

A flash of lightning lit up the forest for a split second, heralding the crack of thunder.

It was time.

Moira dropped her coat from her shoulders as her bones cracked and broke themselves.

She threw her head back, letting the rain pelt her face. She screamed at the heavens.

Moira remembered screaming even as her mind began to fade and her screams turned to a savage howl.

CHAPTER 16

Moira woke up on the soft moss of the forest floor.

She sat back on her heel and lifted a hand to her throbbing forehead, placing the other on her swollen stomach.

She opened her eye and saw the mess that surrounded her.

The shredded corpse of a deer was spread around her. Her hands left her forehead and stomach sticky with the animal's blood.

Moira wiped her bloodied hands on the wet mosses and grass around her and then used her hands to clear the blood from the rest of her body. She rose to her feet and looked around, searching for any clue as to her whereabouts. She wrapped her arms around herself and shivered.

Moira spotted several unusual impressions in the sponge moss to her right. She squatted down next to them.

They were a set of tracks; one was the hoofs of the deer, while the others were much larger and clawed.

The trail led back to her gear.

She enjoyed her stroll through the trees—the grasses

and moss on the forest floor felt soft on her bare feet and the crisp damp air felt good against her skin and in her lungs.

Weaving in and out amongst the trees, it took Moira a few hours to retrace her steps.

She slid on her coat, clutching the cloth close to her body, and then pulled the rest of her gear out from under the thicket. She got dressed in a matter of seconds.

Slipping her axe through her belt, Moira returned to the road and strode towards her freedom.

Moira strode down the rows of carts towards the city gates.

"Did you hear about the Terror?"

Moira froze mid-stride. Two guards were huddled near the guard station, using two cut blocks of wood as seats.

Leaning against the nearest cart, she listened in on their conversation.

"Take another victim did it?"

"Nope."

"Then what is it? Come on, spill it Walsh."

"It's dead."

The other guard waved him off. "Get out of here."

"No, really O'Brien. It's true—Alistair Sand was missing his arm. He claims some woman did the creature in."

The guard sitting in the guard post popped out of the window and balked at him. "A woman killed the thing? Now I know you're yanking us."

Walsh flipped the other man off, sending him back into his wooden box with a laugh.

"Woman or no, I'm glad to hear that thing is gone." O'Brien shook his head. "I've seen enough bits and bobs nailed to that wall."

"I wish Commander Gallagher could have seen this day."

Both of the Trident Bay guards raised an invisible drink to the sky.

"Rest well Commander Gallagher, you poor bastard." Walsh scratched the blond scruff of his beard. "Have you heard about his kids lately?"

"They're doing all right—they visit that wall every day from what I've heard."

A grey-haired guard approached the trio, his sword swung off of his shoulder.

"Eh, Cromwell, did you hear about the Terror?"

"Aye."

"Walsh claims that a woman killed the thing," the guard chimed from inside the shack.

"Aye, it was a woman."

"Oh, come on, you don't believe that shite do you?"

"Of course I do—she's right over there." Cromwell pointed straight at Moira.

Moira pushed off of the cart and approached the group.

"How did you spot me?" Moira asked.

The guards stared at her with mouths held wide. Walsh's face was red.

"Caspian told me to keep my eyes open for you." He drove the point of his sword into the earth beside him and crossed his arms. "That and that coat gave you away, Abalon-lover. Took your sweet time getting back?"

Moira shrugged. "I felt like a walk. Do you know where he is?"

Cromwell snorted. "Aye, he's at his mansion. I sent a messenger there to find him just a moment ago."

Cromwell grabbed her arm as she turned to leave.

"Whoa, Abalon-lover, he specifically told me to escort you to the gate."

She nodded.

"You don't look like one of his regulars," the guard said with a yawn. He was standing on the other side of the gate to Caspian's neighbourhood.

"That's because I'm not. I've been only to his house once."

"That's how it usually goes."

Cromwell laughed behind her as she wrapped her hands around the metal bars.

"Listen, you've seen me with Caspian before," Moira said. "He's looking for me."

"Cromwell," the guard said, "is this true?"

The old warrior nodded.

The man groaned as he pulled the gate open. "His house is th—"

"The yellow one, I know." Moira strode through the gate. "Thank you."

Moira hopped up the steps to Caspian's home and opened his door. She could hear Caspian's familiar salt-water laugh.

"So, is there any proof to any of this lad?"

"Oh absolutely, I saw it all myself. Sir"

Moira closed the door behind her and crept towards the voices. A powerful scent of smoke and soil wafted through the house.

"Really?"

"I was on the firing squad. I almost died. Sir."

She continued down the hall, passing the stairs to the second floor.

"Amazing lad, amazing, and have you shown this to anyone else? The guards at the gate perhaps?"

"No, it took us a while to produce the few copies we have. We were hoping you could copy this one to start printing them yourself. But I'm sure after a few glances that your guardsmen will be able to pick her out of a crowd."

"No need lad, no need. There will be plenty of time to do that later. I'll get the poster into production as soon as possible."

They were just around the corner.

"I'm sure Chieftain Quinn will appreciate this greatly. . ."

Moira froze as the Quinn guard and Caspian rounded the corner.

"If there is anything you ne—" The guard's mouth dropped.

They stared at each other, wide-eyed. The guard made the first move, pulling his pistol, Moira close behind—but it was Caspian who struck first. He slammed the Quinn guard against the wall.

"What the—"

The man's pistol dropped to the floor. His hat swiftly followed as Caspian grabbed the side of his head and slammed it into the wall.

Moira stood in shock as the guard landed on his hands and knees. He struggled to get back to his feet, but Caspian wrapped his arm under the guard's chin and wrenched his head up before twisting it to the side.

A crack jolted the guard's body, sending it into a spasm. With another twist and crack, he fell still.

"Oh my god." Moira kept a white-knuckled grip on her pistol as she covered her mouth.

"Wait, Moira. Hold on a second lass."

She turned and ran for the door.

Caspian ran after her. "Wait!"

Moira reached the door and tried to pull it open, but Caspian grabbed her.

"Let me go!"

"Just wait."

She struggled and kicked, throwing her head against him.

"Why? Why did you do that? You know what I am now. You know, but you killed him. Why? Why him?"

"Calm down lass. I did it to protect you."

She stopped thrashing but continued to struggle in his grip. "Why protect me? Protect me from what? He was a guard; he was an innocent man."

"And so are you. He was going to kill you. You saw it—he was pulling out his gun to shoot you. He was going to kill an innocent person."

"You don't know if he was."

He twisted her around and gripped her by the shoulders, looking her dead in the eye. "Moira, listen to me. Look at the poster. Reach into my pocket—that one right there—and read it."

"He was innocent."

"Read it!"

Moira pulled out the poster and unfolded it. A few of her tears dropped on the drawn portrait, soaking into the rough piece of parchment. Underneath the picture was the order to kill on sight.

She let the poster fall to the ground as she burst into tears. Caspian wrapped his arms around her and held her close to him, letting her muffle her cries in the wool covering his chest.

"Shhhh, it's all right. I can protect you."

Moira used her wrists to push herself off of his chest and pressed her back against the door.

"Protect me? I'm a fucking werewolf Caspian. I turn into a goddamned monster. I tear people apart with my bare hands. How are you going to protect them from me?"

"Did you want him to kill you?"

"What I wanted was to live my life like anyone else, but I couldn't. I wanted to protect the people around me to make up for what I did, but they cast me out. So I left, Caspian. I tried to disappear, to live my life the best I could somewhere else. I didn't want this. I didn't want another innocent life on my hands."

"Life rarely works the way we expect it to, but it works the way it is meant to. In my experience, everything—even tragedy—comes with an opportunity."

Moira thrust her finger towards the corpse.

"Opportunity? You think there is an opportunity here? Look Caspian. Look at him. Tell me what this will bring." She shielded her face with her hands. "I didn't want this."

"Well, you're still alive lass for one; you still have the chance to make the world a better place."

Moira wrapped her arms around her waist and choked back a tear. "Well that's just great. I have no idea how to make anything out of this mess."

Caspian stepped forwards and grasped her hand. "I do."

"How?"

"The whole city has heard about your bout with the Terror. That gives you influence."

"Influence doesn't fix my problem Caspian."

"Not without a little creativity."

"Really? Then what about Quinn? They have a bounty out on my head."

"I'll grant you sanctuary. He won't care about you as long as you stay out of his county."

"And the people of Trident Bay? What are you going to do once they find out what I am? They weren't happy with the Terror stalking about. I doubt they'll be happy about having a new monster to worry about."

"You've lived amongst the people of Quinn before and didn't kill anyone? You must be able to control it."

"And what if I can't anymore?"

"I know everything about this is complicated lass, but I'll work it all out. Trust me."

Moira shook her head. "No. No! You agreed to get me into Qesuis. I held up my end of the bargain, you need to hold up yours."

She turned towards the door, but Caspian caught her hand.

"Wait, Moira—there are still two more full moons, are there not?"

"Yes."

"And you'll turn during each?"

She nodded her head.

"Well then, I guess you have nowhere to go for the next two days anyways. Even if I did sail you out to Qesuis this very moment."

Moira removed her hand from the door.

"What's your point?"

"My point is, you're going to change anyways, you may as well let me try to help you."

"And get you killed in the process? I don't want any more blood on my hands."

Caspian waved the hat in front of her.

"The bodies seem to be piling up whether you want them to or not."

A tear trailed down Moira's face. She slapped him across the face. She grabbed and turned the handle.

"Moira, wait." He grabbed her wrist. She swung around and slapped him again in his reddened cheek. "Look, I'm sorry, all I meant was you don't kill innocents, right?"

"Never."

"Well what about killers? You'd avenge someone right?"

"I suppose I would."

Caspian turned to the side and pointed the hat down the hall to the body of the guard.

"Avenge him then. Let me help you get control of yourself. If I win, then you get control; if I lose, then you get justice for your friend over there. I'll even tell the captain of my ship to take you wherever you want if I turn up dead."

Moira held the side of her head. "Fine, all right. We'll try."

Caspian clapped his hands together. "Perfect."

"What are you going to do about him?" Moira pointed to the corpse.

"Teague would appreciate a human body to experiment with."

"And how are you going to get there?"

"The guards know how to be discrete when I need them to."

Moira opened the door and stepped out with Caspian behind her. She took a deep breath in and out.

"I need to get out of here for a while. Clear my head."

"Well, I need to make a trip to the market district anyway, but after do you want to go get something to eat?"

Moira placed a hand on her stomach. "I don't feel hungry."

CHAPTER 17

"Teague is going to handle the situation back home."

Caspian trotted down the steps of Apothecary's End with the Quinn guard's hat tucked underneath his arm. He slid up to Moira, threading his hand through her arm and around her back.

"What's next in your plan?"

"I don't know about you, lass, but I'm starving. How about we swing by the Windwake for something—what do you think lass?"

"Seems fine by me."

"Well then, we have that issue of yours to deal with tonight. No time to waste lass!"

He removed his hand from her and ran up beside an empty cart. Grabbing hold of the back of the wagon, he hoisted himself into the cart and sat with his legs dangling off the edge. He held out his hand towards Moira as the cart bounced away from her. She sprinted after him and grabbed his hand. He pulled her into the wagon to sit beside him.

"So, tell me Moira, how did you come to be what you are?"

Moira frowned at him then turned to the driver of the wagon. The man had his back to them with his head pointed squarely ahead of him. If he was listening to their conversation, he wasn't showing it.

"What do you think happened? I got bit," she whispered.

"Of course lass, but how? And how did you survive the attack?"

"I don't think this is the place to talk about that kind of thing."

"Nobody is going to hear you. I told you my life story; now you tell me yours."

She sighed. "It bit into my shoulder fourteen years ago. It did this to me too." She mimicked a slashing motion across the left side of her face.

"Really? How did you escape?"

Moira paused for a few seconds and stared at the running road beneath her feet.

"I shot it in the face and saved myself."

Caspian laughed. "You shot it in the face?"

"Yes."

"With what?"

Moira went to tug on her blunderbuss's strap but found nothing. "With the gun I lost."

"Is this story true?"

"True enough."

Caspian laughed. "True enough? Is that all I'm going to get out of you? Just what's true enough?"

"That's all you're going to get."

"Well, we all have our secrets lass, we all have secrets—but yours is a particularly interesting secret, isn't it? One with a story worth telling."

Moira turned away from him and wrapped her arms

around herself. "It's not some made-up story, it's my past —there were consequences to what happened. It's something I don't want to remember, but I can't forget. I'm sure as hell not going to share it. I'm pretty sure people who confess that kind of thing end up at the end of a firing squad pretty damn quick. Why should I share anyway?"

"Fair enough lass, fair enough, but I can see it in your eyes. Keeping it locked away in there is killing you." He tapped his finger against her head, making her wrinkle her brow. "You want to tell somebody what happened. I know you do."

"I thought about telling someone once." Moira shook her head and narrowed her eyes at him. "But why should that person be you?"

He shrugged. "I'm curious and I can keep a secret." He winked. "I've heard the tales of hundreds of different people over the years in a dozen different taverns in a dozen different ports: war stories, love stories, stories about the Red Wave . . . I've heard them all. But yours is unique; out of all those people who I've met, you're special. Oh, here we are."

Caspian hopped off of the wagon and almost fell backwards as his feet touched the main dock road. Moira hopped off a split-second later and grabbed his shoulder to steady herself.

Moira let go of his shoulder and wrapped her arms around herself.

Caspian turned to her and grasped her by the shoulders.

"Moira, I knew it the moment I saw you that there was something unique about you. By the spirits lass, you've killed the Terror of Trident. You possess a strength I've never seen before."

Moira smiled up at him. She could feel the heat in her face.

Caspian let her go and strode off towards the memorial.

Moira followed beside him. "Caspian, where are you going?"

He glanced over his shoulder. "I'm going to nail this up."

"The Terror is dead."

Caspian stopped in front of the board and pulled the hat out from under his arm. He drummed his fingers against the brim of the hat as he searched for a spot for the new addition. Moira touched his shoulder.

"No one is going to believe the Terror killed the guard."

"No, but they'll believe he died in an accident." He turned to her. "I've made a decree to keep the memorial; not only to commemorate the victims of the Terror, but to remember anyone who's met an untimely fate." He shook the hat. "Like our friend here."

"Have you used this trick before?" She grabbed his arm. "Caspian, were all the people on this wall killed by the Terror?"

"Keep your voice down lass. As far as everyone is concerned, everyone on this wall is a victim of the Terror."

"Is that a no?"

"Remember, death can bring opportunity," he grunted as he yanked a nail holding a torn piece of sweater out of the wall. Holding the hat over the hole left behind by the nail, Caspian pushed the nail through the brim of the hat and into the hole, leaving the multicoloured piece of wool on top. "What do you think?"

"I think there're too many."

Caspian reached his arm around her shoulder and squeezed her. "I know, I know. At least the beast won't be adding any contributions—thanks to you. All of these trin-kets . . . they're in the city's past. It's the future we need to concern ourselves with right now. Speaking of which"—he turned and walked with her back down the road—"I need a drink."

"Have one for both of us."

The crowds swerved around them as they passed, nodding and greeting Caspian. He waved and gave pats on the back.

Moira shielded her face from them all.

Caspian whispered in her ear. "Why are you hiding?"

"Under the circumstances, I don't think it is a smart idea to be parading myself in front of people."

"It's fine lass, none of them know a thing."

"How do you know? Any one of them could be from Quinn or could have seen one of those posters."

"Then why do you keep wearing the same damn hat everywhere? They even have you wearing that hat in the portrait."

Caspian laughed as Moira yanked the hat of her head and clutched it against her chest.

"It's important to me."

"Oh stop your worrying, no one is going to shoot you dead in the street." He stopped in front of the doors to the Windwake, plucked the hat from Moira's hands, and popped it back on top of her head. "Those posters are for the guard and the guard only. Since none of them have seen it, there's nothing to be afraid of. I've got the only copy right here." He tapped the pocket of his vest.

Moira let out a sigh and straightened her hat as Caspian led her into the inn.

"Hello my friends!" He raised his hand above his head.

Half of the people in the building turned to them and

cheered. The other half looked in their direction but quickly lost interest.

Captain Toal rushed up to them with a group of other enthusiastic patrons and clasped Caspian by the arm. "Good to see you, boss."

Caspian returned the gesture with a laugh. "How goes the hunt for Plunkett, Captain?"

"He's a slippery bastard, but we're closing in on him." The guard captain cracked his knuckles. "I'm looking forward to getting my hands on him—he's got a lot to answer for."

He looked at Moira and smiled with his blackened teeth. "I remember you. You helped put down that rally, what was it, four days ago?"

Caspian raised an eyebrow. "You helped the captain?"

Toal laughed. "Absolutely, she even shot two of them. Pissed the lot right off."

Caspian smirked. "Really?"

Moira frowned. "I shot them, but I didn't kill them."

"They would have deserved it though. Those filthy bastards." Toal spat a black glob on the ground.

Caspian squeezed Toal's shoulder. "I have some ideas we should discuss later, but for now"—he raised his hand into the air and grinned—"lets drink."

The crowd roared their approval and the waitresses sprang into action. Caspian let go of Moira and sat on top of a table, one leg hanging off its end while the other perched on the seat next to him. Moira took a seat in a chair beside him while the crowd gathered around him.

"All right lads, lasses—as all of you have heard, the Terror has been slain."

A few of the patrons clapped.

"Yes, the creature's reign of terror is over and we have

this woman to thank for it." Caspian reached over and gave Moira's shoulder a shake.

The patrons sitting at their own tables turned their heads to her.

Moira stared at the crowd with a frown.

"Oh don't be shy lass, introduce yourself. The people want to know who you are."

Moira turned to stare Caspian in the eye. "I really don't think that is a good idea."

"Come on, they all want to know." He turned to the crowd. "You want to know who this brave woman is don't you?"

"Her name's Moira isn't it?" yelled one man.

"How did you kill it?" yelled another.

He leaned and whispered to her. "They already know your name. Here's your chance to show them you aren't a monster, you're a hero." He leaned back and raised his arms to the crowd. "Come on, they're all waiting."

Moira sat there, her legs crossed, staring at the numerous faces looking at her in anticipation. With a heavy breath, she rose from her seat and stood next to Caspian.

"My name is Moira, Moira Ashe. I'm sorry for my . . . hesitation. I don't usually speak in front of crowds like this, but I'm glad you are all safe from that creature now."

The crowd grew as patrons left their tables to join the gathering.

Servers emerged from the kitchen with trays of bottles and glasses filled with a multitude of different-coloured liquids. The girls marched towards the crowd, and many patrons rushed to meet them halfway.

The blonde serving girl rushed up to Caspian. "I made sure to save two of your favourites Caspian."

Caspian gave her a nod. He pulled out his axe and

rested it across his knee before grabbing the last two bottles off of her tray. "Thanks Orla."

She stood, swaying back and forth with her tray clutched in both of her hands.

Caspian sat one of his bottles next to him while he slid the axe head down the neck of the other bottle, knocking the cork out and sending it spinning over the heads of the crowd. He passed it to Moira. "Here, drink up."

Moira shook her head. "I can't drink."

"Take it."

She pushed the bottle away. "I don't want it."

Caspian pulled the bottle away. "More for me then."

"I wouldn't mind one Caspian," Orla said.

He smiled and passed the open bottle to her.

Caspian opened his second bottle and took a drink of his whiskey then shouted at the crowd: "I don't know about all of you, but I would love to hear how the Terror died."

Several members of the crowd nodded their heads and muttered their agreement.

"Right then Moira, tell us the tale." He held out his hand to her. "Come up here where they can all see you."

Moira accepted his hand and stood before the crowd. She stared at the anticipation-filled faces of the people surrounding her. Taking a deep breath, she cleared her throat.

"I was told that the creature might target a ship, *The Fortune's Tide*, by Kevin Corcoran. I joined the crew hoping to slay the beast."

"Were you scared?" Caspian asked.

"Not really, I knew what I was facing. It wasn't my first fight with it."

"What happened?" Caspian took a bite of his lamb and washed it down with a drink of whiskey.

"It killed half of Alistair Sand's crew and tore off Alistair's arm before it finally died."

"And you went on the voyage to help the people of Trident Bay, didn't you lass?"

She hesitated for a second. "I did."

"You would die to protect the people of Trident Bay, to free them from fear. Wouldn't you, lass?"

"I almost did die. In our first fight, it sprayed water at me from its mouth. It blinded me, I could barely fight back. The same happened to the crew."

"Tell it from the beginning. We want details," added Caspian.

"It was very late in the evening; the sky was dark. That's when it attacked. It surprised us at first, crawling onto the boat and grabbing one of the crewmen. I shot the Terror, but it killed him anyway."

"Come on Moira, details." Caspian beckoned to her with his hand and took a drink.

Moira shook her head. "I don't think anyone wants to hear about that."

Many of the people in the group shook their heads.

Caspian shrugged. "Fine. What happened next?"

"It came at me and another member of the crew. It threw me off of the boat. By the time I made it back on board, the crewman was dead."

The crowd frowned.

"That's also when captain Alistair Sand and his crew came up from the lower deck."

"And that's when they were sprayed," Caspian said.

"That's when they were sprayed. The Terror was going to kill them while they were blinded, but I got to it first."

"Got to killing them?" a member of the crowd asked.

"What? No, no, I got to the siorclan first."

103

He laughed. "Of course, of course, keep going."

"I hurled my axe into its back and we fought toe to toe. It leapt on me and tried to crush me, but I forced it back by stabbing it in its arm. That's when it attacked the captain and took his arm. I tried fighting it again, which spared the captain's life, but the Terror disarmed me."

"But not like how it disarmed Alistair." Caspian smirked at her while members of the crowd laughed.

Moira glared at him. "The poor man lost his arm and half his crew, Caspian, don't joke about it."

Caspian patted her shoulder. "You're right, I'm sorry. I won't make any more jokes."

"Thank you." She turned back to the crowd. "I lost my weapons, but I managed to grab a blunderbuss that had been dropped by one of the crewmen when they were sprayed by the Terror."

"The water made the gun not work," Caspian said.

"I used it as a club at first, but one of the crew drove a spear into the siorclan's side. The beast killed her, but it gave me enough time to dry the weapon. When it charged back at me, I shot it. A dozen rounds tore through the bastard, spilling its blood all over the deck, and it fell overboard."

Caspian clapped. "That sounds like the story of a hero. Am I right?"

The crowd clapped with him.

"Bullshit!" called a man.

The clapping faded as the crowd looked around for the speaker.

Caspian searched the group. "Who said that? Let him forward."

A man pushed his way to the front of the crowd and scratched at his patchy beard. "You think killing some stupid beast makes you a hero? There are people suffering in this city."

"Those people made their choice when they backed Plunkett," Caspian said.

The man stomped his foot and balled his fists. "You can't take away someone's job just because they didn't vote for you."

Captain Toal took a step forward, but Caspian gestured for him to stop.

"What is he talking about Caspian?" Moira asked

"There were only so many jobs available, so I made sure that those who'd supported me were looked after."

"And anyone who didn't vote for him was sent to the poor district with Plunkett," the man shouted. "Whoreson, tyrant." He spat on Caspian's vest.

Caspian shook with rage as the crimson glob slid down his chest.

"You're going to regre—"

Toal punched the man, throwing him to the ground. Orla ran up and kicked the man alongside Toal.

Some members of the crowd gasped while others jeered and egged on the beating.

Moira leapt down and rushed to the man, pushing the other woman and the guard captain back. "Stop."

Orla scurried back to Caspian's side, but Toal held his ground, glaring at Moira with closed fists.

"Enough Liam." Caspian gestured towards the door. "Toss the bastard out."

The guard captain reached down and pulled the bloodied man to his feet. Caspian slipped off his soiled vest and handed it to Orla. With a smile, she bounded off to the kitchen, garment in tow.

Toal hauled the man to the door and threw him outside. Spitting on the man, he turned and marched back to the group. "Is that everything you wanted?"

The wanted poster in Caspian's vest. Moira felt her stomach drop.

Caspian shook his empty bottle. "I'd like another drink—"

"I'll get it for you," Moira said.

Caspian smirked. "Hurry back, I'm going to tell the story of my first fight with the Terror."

Moira rushed to the kitchen.

The kitchen was filled with cooks and servants, but Orla was nowhere to be seen.

Moira scrambled down the hall, searching every room she passed.

She found Orla standing alone in a small room. She was standing perfectly still, the poster stretched open in her hands, her eyes wide.

She saw Moira.

Orla's face went pale as Moira ripped the paper from her hands. She ripped the poster into pieces before soaking them in the basin of water next to her.

Orla's mouth moved but she was silent.

"Stay right here and don't tell anyone." Moira pulled out a knife. "Not a single person."

Orla stood frozen as Moira ran back down the hall.

The crowd before Caspian had shrunk considerably. Most had returned to their own tables or had left the inn completely.

"I could smell the stink of rotten fish on his breath and I could feel the spray from the water that churns in his gut."

Caspian pulled up his sleeve, revealing scars on his arm. "That's where I got these—oh, there you are, where's the whisky?"

Moira whispered to him. "Orla knows."

"Orla is bringing the drink then?"

She shook her head "You need to come with me right now."

"I'm right in the middle of my story."

Moira squeezed his leg. "She found the poster."

Caspian's eyebrows rose as he cursed.

He raised his voice to the crowd. "All right everyone, Moira and I have to go now, but remember to tell everyone about our new hero. Let's hear it for Moira, lads."

"To Moira Ashe, protector of Trident Bay!"

She smiled and thanked the crowd then took off towards the kitchen.

Caspian sighed and followed her.

Orla was still standing next to the basin. The colour returned to her face as Caspian entered the room.

Orla pointed at Moira. "Caspian, she's a fucking werew—"

Caspian cupped his hand over her mouth. "I know." He held a finger up to his mouth then removed his hand from hers.

Orla stared wide-eyed at Moira.

Caspian put his hands on her shoulders. "You need to keep this quiet. You can't tell anyone."

"She'll kill people Caspian." Her mouth fell open. "She's in your house."

"She's not going to hurt anyone."

"She's a werewo—"

He cupped his hand over her mouth again. "By the spirits lass, keep your voice down."

Moira could feel the sweat on her forehead. "She's going to tell everyone."

"Where is the poster?"

Moira pointed to the basin of water filled with Caspian's vest and the blotched remains of the poster.

Caspian thought for a few seconds before taking his hand off of Orla's mouth. "Everything will be fine."

Moira's gave him a sideways glance. "What?"

"Orla has no evidence; no one will believe her."

Orla glared at Caspian. "I'm not going to share a roof with a beast." She pointed at Moira. "It's her or me."

"Orla, you need to understand: Moira is special."

She slapped Caspian across the face. "Are you fucking her?"

His hands squeezed her shoulders. "I didn't mean it like that. I meant that I need her."

Tears welled up in her eyes. "Have her then." She tried to shake out of his grasp.

"Hold on lass."

She slapped him again, then again.

He let go of her and let her storm off.

"What do you mean you need me?" Moira said, stepping towards Caspian.

Caspian shook. "Let's just get out of here."

"What did you mean?"

With a roar, he threw the basin to the ground, spilling the water and his vest on the ground.

Moira took a step back.

He let out a slow breath then cleared his throat. "You're the hero of Trident Bay now. That gives you influence, power. Someone is trying to usurp me Moira, and they're going to try using you to do it. I need you to help me stop that." He turned to her. "I'll help you get to Qesuis; you fulfilled your end of the bargain, but I need your help again." He held out his hand. "I'll help you with your condition regardless of your answer."

Moira looked at his hand for several seconds before shaking it. "Deal."

Caspian smiled. "Perfect, lass."

CHAPTER 18

Moira and Caspian walked side by side down the dockside road.

"Why did you have me tell a story to those people Caspian? Now they all know my name and they saw my face. You even told them to spread it around, and now Orla knows what I am. Are you crazy?"

"Just let me explain myself, all right lass?"

Moira turned her eye to look at Caspian. "I'll listen."

"You see, I've learned a lot about people these last few years, and one of the things I learned is about controlling people's perceptions. You want to live in peace, don't you?"

She nodded.

"Well, you can have that right here, but to do that you have to get to the people first, before Ryan Quinn does. You need to be seen by them, you need to be embraced by them."

"Why does that matter? Quinn is a chieftain; why would they believe me over him?"

Caspian gave her a devilish smile. "Well, who just proclaimed you a hero of Trident Bay?"

"You did."

"People will believe the first thing they are told and it takes one hell of a convincing argument to change their minds. You just told a story about how you risked your life for these people, and you were backed up by the most trusted man in the city. They have everything they need to stand by you. If you were skulking around in the shadows and Ryan showed up, what do you think they would do?" He gave her a wink. "You're one of us now, and that means everything."

Moira stared at him, mouth open. "Are you trying to manipulate them?"

He shook his head. "Not manipulating—I'm telling them the truth before someone else can tell them another truth. If that happens to make the people not believe the other person's truth"—he shrugged his shoulders—"then that's just too bad."

"Do you really think that I'll be safe from Quinn now?"

"For now, lass, no one will believe a word of that werewolf nonsense. But I will warn you: people's minds can be changed by first-hand evidence. So keep the shapeshifting out of the city and everything will be fine."

Moira sighed. "I guess it's not like I haven't told lies to protect myself before."

"You're not getting it Moira; we're not lying. Everything we've said is true."

"It feels wrong."

Caspian threw his hands up in frustration. "Wrong? Do you know what is really wrong? Ordering a death sentence for someone who is trying to save people. That's what's wrong." He took a breath and began rubbing her arms and shoulders again. "Listen Moira, I know this isn't exactly

111

what you wanted, but trust me, it's the best you could hope for."

"I know, I'm sorry. You're just trying to help me and you've done so much for me already. Thank you. I really mean that."

"You're welcome, but there is still that matter we have to take care of tonight."

CHAPTER 19

"I wasn't looking lass, honest," Caspian said, facing the crumbling brick wall of the ancient tower. A small rock careened across the moonlit arena, bouncing off of his shoulder. Caspian shrugged off the hit.

"Liar! I just saw you turn around." Moira picked up another rock, using her other hand to hold the blanket draped over her shoulders.

"I was just making sure you weren't turning, that was all."

"If I was turning, you would know. Just keep looking at that wall."

Caspian let out a sigh and turned around. "Is this all necessary? Look lass, it's not like I can see anything . . . well, not much with that sheet of yours." He dodged the rock that sailed by his head. "I have seen naked women before."

The rock clacked against the wall and fell into the pile of Moira's gear.

"It's not just about that. Not really." Moira used both of her hands to pull the blanket tight around her as she turned away from Caspian. "This is the first time I've voluntarily let someone be present for this."

A sack sat open in front of her, revealing the half-dozen pieces of swine.

Caspian took a step towards her with an eyebrow raised. "Voluntarily?"

"Yes, voluntarily. Why do you think Quinn is hunting me in the first place? A man named Lincoln Clarke saw me turn. He reported me to Quinn, who had me thrown in jail where I shapeshifted in a cell guarded by half a dozen people."

"Lincoln Clarke? The name doesn't sound Fotish to me. It sounds Abalonian"

"He actually is from Abalon."

"Is he? What was an Abalonian doing so far east?"

"He came to me looking for information."

"Information on what?"

"He wanted to know about werewolves. How to hunt them and whatnot."

"Well, he found the right lass for that. You have a lot of first-hand experience."

"Why? Because I hunted them or because I am one?"

"Both."

"I guess Lelagh was smiling down on him that day, because he got the hunter and the monster." She glanced over her shoulder at Caspian. "Hey, back to the wall. You want to be as far away from me as possible."

Caspian walked backwards away from Moira until he touched his back to the wall. "So, you did help him."

Moira nodded. "I did."

"Any particular reason why you helped him, lass? Seems to me that handing out that kind of information wouldn't be in your best interest." He tilted his head. "Why teach someone how to hunt you?"

"He wasn't trying to hunt me exactly, he was trying to stop the spread of werewolves across Abalon."

"Was he telling the truth?"

Moira shrugged. "I don't know; I don't see how useful that knowledge would be to him otherwise."

"Anyway lass, did you tell him everything you knew?"

"I didn't tell him everything I knew, I just told him enough so that he had something useful to bring back home. He was going to use it to help people somewhere very far away from me. I didn't see any harm in it." Moira smiled to herself. "And he paid me, so there was that."

Caspian laughed. "Well, at least you didn't do it for free."

Moira hung her head. "It almost cost me everything though. He ended up exposing me. Seven years I lived in Quinn—seven years! Then he shows up and destroys everything."

"Did you kill him for it?"

Moira swung around, causing the blanket to open a small amount. "No! I know I felt betrayed and angry with him, but I can't blame him for what he did. I was the one who made my living from hunting and exposing people who were just like me. What happened to me I've done a dozen times over to other people." She pulled the blanket closed once she noticed Caspian's wandering eye and turned back around.

Caspian leaned against the wall and tapped the head of his axe against his boot in a steady rhythm while Moira sat watching the moon climb higher and higher into the night sky.

"How did you escape from Quinn?"

"Didn't that guard tell you?"

"He told me some of what happened. He said you broke out of jail as a werewolf and then rampaged through the town, but he never said how you actually escaped Quinn."

"They let me out the front gate."

Caspian's beat stopped dead. "They want you dead, but they just let you walk out the front gate?"

"Lincoln helped me do it."

Caspian pushed himself off of the wall. "The man who exposed you was the same man who helped you escape? I've heard a lot of stories, but that I find hard to believe lass."

"He had a change of heart and helped me escape."

Caspian paced back and forth, his axe resting on his shoulder. "Why did he change his mind?"

Moira shrugged. "He said that I was a good person, that I didn't deserve what had happened to me . . . he told me that I was special."

Caspian stopped pacing and leaned against the wall again. "Well, sounds like he knew you pretty well."

Moira smiled. "I never got to thank him for getting me out of Quinn. I also never got to apologize for holding a knife to his throat or for kicking him into the mud."

"Maybe you'll see him again."

Moira shook her head. "I would have liked to—he's a good-hearted man—but he's probably halfway to Abalon by now."

"You never know lass, you could send a letter to Abalon and hope it finds him."

Moira turned to him and laughed. "Do you think that would—" Moira cried out in pain as one of her bones cracked.

Caspian jumped off of the wall and rushed towards her.

Moira held her palm out at him. "Stop, I'll be okay—just keep back."

Caspian backed away slowly as Moira was driven to her hands and knees, letting the sheet drape freely off of her shoulders.

"Deep breaths lass."

"This isn't my . . . my first . . ."

Her arms and legs shifted and warped, pushing her onto her side. Her heavy breaths turned to snarls as her body grew larger. Her claws dug into the soil beneath her, which squeezed between her fingers. She pushed herself into a squat, letting the blanket slide off of her hunched frame. She tore at the sack of meat.

"Oh ho! You are a beauty Moira, just look at you!"

She heard Caspian's words, but they sounded distant and muffled. She looked up at him and bared her teeth.

"Whoa now lass, you're still in there, I know you are. Just focus on that beast in your head—feel it, embrace it. Don't just hold it back; make it a part of you."

She felt tired and confused, but she tried to do as Caspian instructed. She pulled against the beast that was wresting for control of her body and tried to feel the other in her head. As she searched inside herself, her control slipped.

She stepped forwards towards Caspian, claws held ready to tear him to pieces.

Caspian reached down beside him and picked up a blunderbuss. He pulled back the hammer. "Hold it right there, lass."

Moira returned her focus to fighting for control. Throwing her head to the sky and tossing it from side to side, she let out a howl as her two sides fought. She stopped the other's advance but failed to triumph over the beast. She

117

was only able to hold it back for a few seconds before her exhaustion forced her to let go. She tried to yell, to tell Caspian to get away, but all of it came out as growls and snarls. She surged towards Caspian.

Caspian pointed the gun towards her and pulled the trigger. An explosion of rounds flew towards her legs. The balls of lead punched into her flesh. Moira collapsed on the ground. Her right leg was shredded, the blood coating her black coat. She howled in pain.

"I'm sorry about that lass, but you need to get a grip on yourself. That beast in your head is just another part of you. You need to explore it, integrate it." He hooked the weapon in the crook of his arm and threaded his fingers together.

Moira felt herself starting to fade amongst the fury of rage and pain swirling in her head. She growled and pulled herself towards Caspian using her two front limbs.

"Hold on now Moira."

Caspian scrambled to reload the weapon, but as she dragged herself closer, he abandoned the effort and slung the blunderbuss over his shoulder. Snatching two pistols from the pile of Moira's gear, he fired them one after another into her left shoulder.

Her left arm collapsed underneath her, halting her progress. She lay on the ground breathing heavy, her good arm stretched forwards, its claws sunk in the soil at Caspian's feet. She snarled in frustration.

Caspian gave her a wide berth as he circled around her, inspecting the state of her injuries. He crouched near her leg and poked at the fusing wounds with a nearby stick.

"By the spirits." He jumped to his feet and ran back to stand in front of her snout. He towered over her, her blunderbuss held in his hands, the butt of the weapon aimed at her head. "I'm sorry about this lass, but we're going to have to continue this tomorrow night. That leg of yours is healing fast and—"

Moira lunged forwards and pushed Caspian to the ground. Using her good hand, she grabbed Caspian's foot. Caspian gripped at the ground around him as Moira pulled him towards her. He stomped at her snout with his free foot. She snapped at his boot, but Caspian kicked her in the side of her head.

"Wake up Moira, I need your help!"

Moira felt the other's grip slip. She surged into the void and took control again. She released Caspian's foot, letting him scramble to his feet, and then struggled to stand on her newly healed leg.

Caspian breathed heavily and retreated to the broken wall.

She lunged towards him.

He lifted himself on top of the tower wall and pulled himself out of her reach. Moira slammed into the stone wall and grabbed the edge, pulling herself closer to Caspian. She snapped her jaws at his feet, struggling to lift herself closer to him.

Caspian pulled his feet away and used both of his hands to pry a brick from the wall. Hoisting the stone over his shoulder, he threw the brick at her.

The brick collided with Moira's head, dazing her for a second. He pried another from the wall and threw it, hitting her in the head again.

Moira's head ached. She slid off of the wall and landed on all fours. She closed her eye and emitted a low growl. Another brick smashed against her, dropping her to the ground.

She opened her eye, but a fog of pain blurred her vision. She saw the dark shadow of Caspian tower over her. She struggled to get to her feet, fighting through the pain in her head. She could hear Caspian's soothing hush. "Shhhhhh. Don't get up lass, just go to sleep now. We'll try again tomorrow."

She saw the shadow strike out, causing an explosion of pain through her skull. She tried once more to struggle to her feet, but Caspian struck again.

She felt the pain, then blacked out.

CHAPTER 20

Moira opened her eye.

She sprung up into a sitting position and threw her head back and forth as she looked around her. The first thing she noticed was the dull ache that sat and throbbed in her skull. The next was the dusty, elaborately patterned walls that surrounded her.

She was sitting in her bed at Caspian's estate. A new hat and coat hung near the door to her room, while her old ones were neatly leaned against the wall underneath with the rest of her equipment.

The new hat was black with a wide brim while the coat was much shorter than her old one, ending at the hip.

Moira looked down and found herself dressed in the clothes gifted to her by Caspian. She pulled at the fabric and reached up to her face, finding her patch still tightly pressed against her eye. She fell back into the embrace of her bedding.

The light of the morning sun beamed down upon her, adding to the warmth of the thick blanket she pulled up to her chin and the half-dozen pillows that surrounded her head.

The scent of fresh sea air seeped through the window, falling gently onto her face.

She took a deep breath of the cool air and held it for a few seconds, letting the salt sting her nostrils before she let it back out again. She snuggled herself further into her bed. She felt like lying there forever, never moving from her cloth cocoon.

She lay there for several minutes, drifting on the edge of sleep, but a knock on her door forced her eye open.

"Come in."

The door creaked slowly open. An older woman peeked into the room, her apron covered with spots of grease.

"I'm sorry to wake you Ms. Ashe, but your breakfast is waiting for you downstairs."

"Is Caspian here?"

"He's waiting for you at the breakfast table. He sent me to fetch you before I took off home."

"Could you tell him I'll be down in a minute?"

"Yes miss, but don't wait too long, your breakfast is getting cold."

"Thank you."

The door closed with a gentle click.

Moira sighed and stared at the ceiling for a second before gripping the corner of her blanket and throwing it aside, exposing her to the morning breeze.

She shivered and swung her legs over the side of the bed and sat hunched over with her head in her hands. Letting out a groan, she pushed herself to her feet. A wave of light-headedness washed over her, blackening her vision and causing her to wobble on her feet. Placing her palm against the wall beside her, she steadied herself before walking to the door and slipping her feet into her boots.

She held her old coat in front of her and then looked at her new one. With a shrug, she threw her old coat onto the bed and pulled on her old garment. She snatched the new hat off of the wall and pulled open the door.

The only sound that floated through the house was the faint clatter of dishes. As Moira stepped forwards, her heels clopped against the wood floors.

Moira walked down the stairs. As she walked into the hall, she froze. She was standing on the same spot of stone that the body of the Quinn guard had been. She saw no trace of the murder, but she felt the sickness swirl in her stomach as she stared down the corridor at the house's front door.

"Are you almost here, Moira?" Caspian called.

"Yeah. I . . . I just came down the stairs, just give me a second."

Moira swallowed hard and tried to ignore her illness as she marched forwards through the hall and Caspian's meeting room to the breakfast table.

Caspian sat in his chair with his back to the silent kitchen. He raised his glass to her as she rounded the corner. "There you are Moira. How did you sleep?"

"Well I guess. My head still hurts a little," she said, taking her seat. "I was also surprised to find myself dressed."

"I had to carry you back home here after our little incident last night, so I figured it was best to get you covered up. Carrying you naked through the streets would have raised too many questions."

"Did anyone ask about what happened?"

"A few of the guards by the gate helped me get you into

a carriage, but don't worry about them—like I told you before, they can be discreet when I need them to be." Caspian tapped his finger against his head. "And sorry about the blows to the head lass, I had to get control of you somehow. You would have torn me apart otherwise."

"I know, I'm sorry. I used to have better control over it."

"What kind of control?"

"I could point it, guide it. I could give it a goal for it to pursue . . . does that make any sense?"

"I understand." Caspian shook his head. He motioned to the table between them. "Come on lass, there is more than enough to choose from, fill your plate."

Moira grabbed a plate of pork strips and settled into her seat. "I could fight; I could do what I needed myself to do. Even when I felt like harming someone, I could pull myself away from it. I could still change at will. I had control. It might not have been as much as I wanted, but it was control. After everything that happened in Quinn, I just don't have that power anymore."

"That's not control; all you had was coercion. You could force yourself into obedience, like a dog on a leash. It tries to pull away; you tug it back into place. But what are you going to do now that you've lost that leash?"

"I don't know what you're talking about."

Caspian stood from his seat. "Then why are you eating that pork all of the damn time? All this food and you've touched nothing else."

Moira picked up a strip from the plate, keeping her eye cast down at the pile of pork. "I just like the taste."

Caspian threw the plate against the wall. Moira

flinched as it shattered, scattering meat across the floor. "Don't lie to me lass! I'm trying to help you here. You're using it as a medication, aren't you?"

Moira stared at him for a few seconds before nodding her head. "It helps feed the cravings."

"No wonder you've got no control, look at you. Your mind is broken into so many pieces—how are you supposed to hold yourself together."

"What am I supposed to do Caspian?" Moira snapped back. "Just do nothing? It helped me before."

"Then why doesn't it work now?"

Moira shook her head. "I don't know. I just feel tired and lost, like I don't know what to do or where I'm going." She felt the tears welling up in her eyes.

Caspian crouched down and placed a hand on her shoulder. "It's all right Moira, we can fix this. You just need to make it part of you."

"What if I don't want to? I'm afraid of it Caspian, I'm scared of what it is and what it can do. And if that becomes a part of me, of who I am as a person, what does that make me?"

"That's for you to find out—but if you try to keep that part of you caged, if you don't find the courage to confront it, someone is going to pay the price."

"I know and I tried last night, but I just don't understand what you're saying about all of this. It doesn't make any sense to me."

Caspian frowned. "Whether you like it or not, this beast is a part of you. You've tried so hard to repress it; it's come back with a vengeance. It has needs Moira, needs that are being ignored."

"Then how am I supposed to do this?"

"I'll help you figure it out."

"How?"

Caspian dropped his hand from her face and stood up and gave her a wink. "I have an idea. Finish your breakfast lass and get some fresh air. We'll meet later this evening at the tower."

CHAPTER 21

M oira wandered around the market.

She watched the people as they milled around her. Many ignored her, but those who spotted her face underneath the brim of her new hat smiled and waved.

She smiled and waved back as she strolled.

Maybe she could stay here?

Without the threat of Quinn bearing down on her, and if Caspian could help her get control of the beast inside her, she could see herself living here.

She smiled and held her head high.

A hand grabbed her arm and pulled her to the left.

She planted her feet and pulled back. Alistair Sand released his grip on her. His hair was slicked back and all of his clothes were now fresh. A heavy gold chain dangled from his neck.

With his hand, he beckoned her towards him, wobbling slightly on unsteady legs.

"Alistair, what are yo—"

He held a hook (which he'd replaced his left hand with) up to his lips. "Quickly," he whispered.

Moira followed him into a tailor shop. Headless mannequins were dressed in various garments and were perched on top of shelves stuffed with heaps of folded cloth.

A woman yelled to them from a back room. "I'll be with you in a moment."

Alistair entered a changing room and motioned for her to follow. "In here."

Moira stood with her hands on her hips. "What are you doing?"

He grabbed her hand and pulled her towards the room. "I'll explain in here. Come on, hurry, before he arrives."

"Who?"

"The guard with the sword."

Moira let him pull her into the changing room. "The guard with the sword?"

Alistair drew the curtain closed and let out a breath. "Caspian is having you followed," he whispered as he peeked through the curtain.

A heavy set of boots walked into the store.

The woman called again. "I'll just be a minute."

"By that man." Alistair moved aside to let Moira see her pursuer.

Cromwell stood in the doorway of the shop, his arms folded and his sword in his right hand. He gave the shop a quick scan before tossing his sword over his shoulder with a sigh and marching out of the shop, grumbling to himself.

"Wait here." Alistair slipped through the curtain and tiptoed to the doorway. He leaned out.

A woman walked through a curtain holding a shirt. "Can I help you?" She walked over to a bare-chested mannequin and stuffed the shirt over its shoulders.

"We were just leaving." Alistair waved to Moira.

She pulled the curtain back and joined Alistair.

"Oh, well then, if you're interested in anything you see, we're having a sale tomorrow."

Alistair smiled at the tailor. "We'll keep that in mind. Thank you."

He walked out of the shop with Moira beside him and quickly pulled her down a back alley.

"What the hell is going on Alistair?" Moira stopped in the alley.

He turned to her. "I'm sorry, let me explain. Caspian was having you followed. He did the same to me."

She crossed her arms. "Why?"

"You're an important person now. Who you talk to, where you go—that's important for him to know."

"Where are we going?"

"I have a friend who wants to meet you. He's not far."

"Who?"

"You'll see." He led her down the alley and to the back of a tavern. A set of stairs led down to a basement door. Alistair walked down the stairs and held the door open for her. "In here."

Moira walked into the basement, which led to a long sloping hallway.

Alistair entered and shut the door behind him. He whistled three long notes as he walked forwards.

The entered a storeroom filled with shelves of barrels and bottles. Lanterns hung from the ceiling, casting a warm glow on the two figures waiting for them: Kevin Corcoran and Gaspard.

Moira stepped into the middle of the room as Alistair slipped past her to join the other men. He stood with a slight wobble.

"Why am I here?" Moira said, crossing her arms.

Gaspard cleared his throat and stepped towards her with a hand extended. "I apologise for my rude remarks when we first met."

Moira refused his hand. "What do you want?"

Gaspard let his hand drop back to his side. "We wanted to present you with a proposition. Your slaying of the Terror has made you a very powerful figure in Trident Bay. Caspian used that same influence to seize power, and now we want you to do the same for us."

"Why would I do that?"

Kevin spit on the floor. "Because Caspian is a bastard."

The corner of Gaspard's mouth twitched. "What he is trying to say is that Caspian has become a hindrance to the growth of the city. He seized control of every major business in the city and wields absolute power over the council. Nothing happens without his permission."

Moira shrugged. "Ryan Quinn maintains a similar model and everything is fine."

"But everything is not fine. Ms. Ashe, Caspian has become a tyrant. He's banished everyone who voted against him to the old quarter to rot. I've lived this scenario before: the riots, the outrage . . . we are headed for disaster."

"I was attacked at a rally in the old quarter. I know what you're talking about." Moira frowned. "But what's your solution?"

"We are going to form a new council, with Plunkett representing the poor. Others—Mr. Corcoran here, for example—will also be present on this new council."

The fisherman nodded to her as he grabbed a bottle off of the shelf next to him and pulled the cork.

"Why not just do that now?"

"Because this new council will need to distribute power between the members. There will be no central figure."

"And you can bet your arse Caspian won't like that idea." Kevin took a swig.

"He doesn't even listen to his council; we are nothing more than puppets who carry out his orders."

Moira tilted her head. "Do you think it will work?"

Gaspard nodded. "Plunkett is already on board."

Her eyebrow raised. "You know where he is?"

Gaspard shook his head. "I've only been able to communicate through messages passed through a network of trusted individuals."

Moira put her hands on her hips. "Is there anyone else involved in this?"

"There are others, but you'll forgive me if I don't trust you enough to reveal their identities."

She nodded her head towards Alistair. "How does he fit into all of this?"

Alistair stepped forwards. "In exchange for a ship with a crew and a lucrative shipping contract"—he used his hook to tap his hat and lift the gold chain around his neck towards her—"I can help break Caspian's stranglehold on business, the largest of which is trade. Thanks to the demise of the Terror, our ships can finally sail safely again."

Gaspard nodded. "The death of the beast has also gained Captain Sand and his crew a reputation for dependable, safe shipping that is further eroding Caspian's customer base. Alistair also stands as an example to others who voted against Caspian."

Alistair smiled. "You don't need Caspian's permission to be successful."

"And what's your part in all of this Kevin?"

Kevin took a swig. "Nothing, I just think he's a bastard."

Moira turned back to Gaspard. "Have you tried talking with Caspian about this?"

Gaspard shook his head. "Speak with Caspian about it if you must, but please keep our identities secret. Caspian is a dangerous man, when he feels his grip slipping he gets violent."

Kevin tossed an empty bottle on the ground. "Just look at that dog of his, Toal."

Moira nodded. "I'll keep it in mind, but I don't want any part in this squabble."

"It's too late for that madame." Gaspard bowed. "I look forwards to speaking with again."

Kevin grabbed another bottle. "It was good to see you again lass. Good job on that whole Terror business."

Moira turned and strode up the hall and through the basement door. Alistair grabbed her arm.

"Hold on a minute Moira." A smile was stretched across his pale face. "I never got to thank you for saving me that night, so thank you, and I'm sorry about all of the secrecy. Everyone knows how close you are to Caspian, but I knew it was worth the risk." He tipped his hat to her with his hook. Then he bounced up the stairs and around the corner.

Smiling, she left to meet Caspian at the tower.

CHAPTER 22

"How is this supposed to help me Caspian?"

Caspian dropped a crate to the ground with a clink. Picking two bottles out of his package, he threw one to Moira.

"Well lass, you don't drink, do you?"

She caught the bottle and shook her head. "No."

"And why is that?"

Moira looked up from the bottle to Caspian. "I'm afraid I'll lose control of myself and change. It isn't worth the risk. I get by fine without it."

Caspian clapped. "Congratulations lass, you've done what a million working Fotish men never could, but for the purposes of our little experiment, you're going to need to break that sobriety."

Moira clasped the bottle with both of her hands and placed it into her lap. "You're not just trying to get me drunk, are you?"

"Actually, that's exactly what I'm trying to do."

She frowned.

Caspian shook the bottle in his hand. "Well, not drunk

exactly. It's liquid courage, lass. It'll serve two purposes: first, I'm going to get rid of your fear of drinking and, secondly, I'm going to let you see what it feels like to not be afraid of that beast in your head. So, if you wouldn't mind . . ."

Moira sighed and pulled the cork out of the bottle. She put it up to her lips and threw her head and the bottle upwards. She swallowed mouthful after mouthful of the bitter burning liquid. She coughed and choked as she tossed the empty bottle to the ground.

"Good lass, but slow down a bit, the day is still early. We still have lots of time."

Moira took a deep breath and then held her hand out to Caspian. "Another one."

He nodded and tossed the bottle he had in his hand. She caught it and yanked out the cork.

Moira gestured to the crate of bottles at Caspian's feet. "Are you going to have any?"

He shook his head. "I would love to lass, but I need to keep my wits about me, just in case something does go wrong with you."

Moira stopped drinking.

Caspian lifted the crate and set it down beside Moira. He took a seat on a rock several paces from her. "Just playing it safe lass. You said it yourself: you don't know what will happen, and after last night, I'm not going to risk it." He patted the blunderbuss lying beside him.

She gave him a glare as she raised the bottle to her lips again. The burn and bitterness of the alcohol lessened with every drink, but the scratching in her mind gained a small amount of strength. Finished with another bottle, she threw it onto the ground and bent over to get another one.

"How are you feeling?"

"I feel a little . . . weird, but all right."

Caspian nodded. "So far, so good then."

"Can I ask you a question?"

"Sure lass, go ahead."

"How do you know so much about what's going on inside my head?"

Caspian laughed and patted the rock beneath him. "I suppose we all go through something like this lass. Everyone has their own beast in their head." He tapped his temple. "Desires and urges—it's the same as that beast of yours." He smirked. "Do you understand?"

Moira lowered the bottle into her lap. "I think so."

Caspian pulled his axe from his belt and began tapping the weapon against his boot as he watched Moira casually sample the bottle in her hand. After a few minutes of silence, she finished the drink and threw the bottle to join the rest on the ground between her and Caspian.

They sat for several minutes in silence.

"Why was Cromwell following me today?"

"He's been following you every day since you returned from your voyage. It's his job to keep an eye on you." He chuckled. "And let me tell you Moira, he's begging me to give him a different assignment."

"Why?"

"He said something about how your fondness for Abalon boils his blood and how it's a pret—"

"No, why does he need to keep an eye on me?"

"Oh, well, because I'm waiting for those usurpers to try meeting with you." He smirked. "Like they did today."

"How do you know?"

"When all of my guards lose track of their targets at the same time, I can put two and two together." He tapped the axe against the stone. "So, what is our dear Gaspard planning with Alistair?"

"They're trying to solve the old quarter problem."

"And how do they plan on doing that?"

"They plan on bringing Plunkett onto the council to represent the poor."

Caspian rubbed his chin for several seconds. "That won't work."

Moira frowned. "Why not?"

"Any suggestion he gives I won't be able to act on. It would defeat the purpose of sticking them there in the first place."

Moira's eyebrows lowered. "You shouldn't be putting anyone anywhere."

"I had to give priority to those who supported me, and I had to give the others a reason to change their minds."

"Gaspard and Alistair don't support you."

"Once I uncover the rest of Gaspard's cohorts, they'll find themselves in the old quarter. As for Alistair, I can't do anything about him." Caspian gave her a devilish smile. "Yet."

"What is that supposed to mean?"

"His business will fail eventually, I promise you that." He rested his head on his hand. "Was there anything else?"

Moira wobbled a little. "They want to form a new council with the power distributed between them."

He laughed. "Stupid bastards."

She glared at him. "What's wrong with that?"

Caspian leaned back. "It will take forever for them to do anything—they'll be constantly bickering, trying to push their own agendas." He pointed his axe towards Trident Bay. "That city has grown leaps and bounds because of my leadership." He patted his chest with the head of the weapon. "My sole leadership. Creative problem-solving, quick decision-making, and a unified pathway forward. That's what my leadership is. If they're opposed to that then maybe you have to ask what their motives are."

"Why does there have to be a struggle at all?" Moira spat. "There seems like plenty of—I don't know—*everything* in the city for everyone. Why does it matter who has what, or who voted for who? Everything could be so much worse for everyone." She threw her hands into the air, tossing some of the alcohol out of her bottle and splashing it on the ground. "Why do we all have to be so selfish?" She pressed her palm to her forehead.

Caspian smirked. "Are you all right lass?"

"What? Oh, I think I'm still all right. My head is feeling . . . a little . . . ah . . . ah, a little . . . I don't know, my thoughts feel like they're floating or swimming. One of those two."

"I think that's about good enough for you, lass. You can stop drinking now."

Moira breathed a sigh of relief. "About time, that is some pretty awful stuff." She tossed her bottle to the ground, causing the remaining liquid to leak out and seep into the ground.

"Look at you, you're six bottles in and still human lass."

Moira smiled and looked down at herself. "Yeah, I guess I am." She held her hand up to her forehead and blinked several times. "The scratching in my head is starting to get worse though."

Caspian used his free hand to pull the gun into his lap. "But you're still okay lass?"

She nodded. "Yeah, yeah. I'm still all right . . ." She groaned and shook her head. "It's just a little hard to concentrate. That's all."

Caspian relaxed and slid the blunderbuss back down beside him. "Are you ready for the next step lass?"

Moira nodded. "I'll try."

Caspian nodded. "All right lass, close your eye."

She took in a deep breath and closed her eye.

"Can you feel the beast?"

She nodded. "I think so."

"What does it feel like?"

Moira squeezed her eye tightly closed. "It feels . . . it feels strong . . ."

"Good lass, strong is good. What else?"

"It feels . . . I don't know . . . it feels . . ."

"What?"

She twisted her head. "Excited."

"Excited?"

"Yes."

"Like it's full of energy perhaps?"

Moira nodded her head. "Yeah, like it wants to be let out."

"Is it coming out?" He gripped the gun.

She shook her head. "No, not yet."

"All right, keep going lass."

She took a deep breath in and held it for a few seconds before letting it back out. "It feels hungry. It feels angry, full of rage. It also feels—oh."

"What?"

Moira felt blood rise in her face. She opened her eye. "Desire."

Caspian raised his eyebrow. "Lust? When was the last time you had sex?" He laughed when Moira squirmed. "Oh, nothing to be embarrassed about lass, just keep going. I think you're close."

She closed her eye again and breathed deep. "It feels . . . it feels . . . I feel . . ."

"Yes? what is it lass?"

She wrinkled her brow. "I feel trapped."

A crack in her arm caused her to yell in pain. She opened her eyes and found Caspian on his feet, her blunderbuss in his arms.

"Are you all right lass?"

She nodded as another crack deformed her other arm.

"Can you stop it?"

She took a breath and closed her eye. She fought through the pain and felt the intense desire for freedom. It swept her up in a rush of emotion. Her bones cracked faster than ever and her flesh began to push against her clothing. She embraced the emotion and made it her own desire. Taking a deep breath, she rode the feeling through, feeling it fade, soothed by her focus. Her body stopped reshaping itself. She kept her breath calm even through the intense agony ripping through her misshapen body. She focused on the feeling and soothed it, letting it fade. Her bones began to break again before returning to their normal shapes.

"Are you all right lass?"

"I'm all right." She winced as she pushed herself into a seating position. "I'm still a little sore."

Caspian wiped the sweat from her brow and stroked her hair. "You did great. You're going to be facing stronger emotions tonight."

"How much longer until then?"

"Still a while yet—get some rest. You'll need it for tonight."

CHAPTER 23

Moira woke up on the soft grass surrounded by the ruined walls of the ancient tower. The deep orange of the dying day painted everything around her with its harsh brush.

"How are you feeling lass?"

Moira groaned. "I'm all right."

She rolled onto her back and stared up into the clear sky.

"It won't be too long now." Moira sprung to her feet, letting her hat tumble off of her head and into the grass. She pulled her gloves off of her hands and tossed them on the ground beside her blanket. "I suppose we'd best get ready then."

Caspian walked over and picked the hat off the ground. He approached Moira as she bent down to pluck the blanket off of the grass.

"There's still another hour before the moon rises."

"And?"

"Is there anything else that you've been afraid to do lass?"

"No."

Caspian tossed her hat beside her feet. "Are you sure you haven't been avoiding something?" Caspian slid his hands around her waist. "Like intimacy?"

Moira looked at him over her shoulder. "I'm not afraid."

Caspian pulled open the buttons holding her coat closed, moving up her body with each strap that gave way. "Then what is it lass?"

She could feel the heat rise in her as he whispered into her ear. He finished splitting her coat apart and pulled it off of her shoulders.

"I couldn't be with anyone without risking them seeing this." Moira slipped her collar over her right shoulder, exposing the scars left by a massive set of jaws.

Caspian let her coat drop to the ground next to her hat and ran his rough hand over her shoulder. "That would raise a number of questions, wouldn't it lass?"

She closed her eye and swayed gently back and forth as Caspian ran his hand over the scar, rubbing his palm against her skin and digging his fingers into her flesh. "People already ask about where the scars on my face came from. How am I supposed to explain the ones on my shoulder?"

He ran his hands down her arms, then her sides, and finally brought them together in front of her stomach. "I understand." He pulled her towards him, pressing his body against her back. "And here I was thinking you didn't like me."

"I didn't like you."

Caspian rubbed his jaw against the side of her neck.

"The first time I saw you, you were yelling and drinking —what was there to like?"

"Usually women like it when I start stirring up the crowd."

"I'm not like other women."

"That's true."

"And you were about two seconds from tearing the dress off of Orla."

"That was also true."

Caspian grabbed the bottom of her shirt. Moira dropped her sheet to the ground and held his hands against her stomach.

"Wait." Moira let a slow breath out. "All right." She helped guide his hands as he pulled the garment up and over her head.

A blast of cold air hit her.

She covered her breasts with her arms. Caspian tossed her shirt to the ground and pressed himself against her.

She felt the warmth of his body and breath on her neck as he ran his fingers down the centre of her chest.

Moira took slow shallow breaths as her arms gave way to him. He traced the outline of her breast. When he reached the pit of her arm, he buried his fingers underneath while his thumb ran over her soft skin.

Moira took in a sudden, sharp breath as he squeezed her chest.

Her breathing quickened as she guided his hands downwards. The tips of his fingers glided down her stomach.

Caspian unbuckled her belt, then tossed it away.

Moira kicked off her boots.

Caspian pulled at the ties of her pants while she wrapped her hands around the back of his head.

She twisted in his grasp as he yanked the string loose. She pressed her chest against his.

He slipped his hands over the fabric and her hips. Caspian slid her pants down with his thumb.

They dropped to her ankles.

Caspian ran his hands up and down her backside. He pulled her closer to him by her waist. She pulled back from him and let both of them breathe a few heavy breaths.

Slight wisps of steam rose from her as her hands slipped down his chest. "I'm sorry Caspian."

"Why?"

"I want to be with you, but I could shift at any moment."

Caspian let her go as Moira pushed away from him.

She turned, dipped down, and threw the sheet over her shoulders. Using one hand to clasp the sheet around her, she pulled Caspian in and kissed him one last time.

Caspian reached up and flipped open the clasp of her patch before pulling it off of her head.

With a sigh, Caspian let the patch drop from his grasp and dropped onto his rock chair. Moira pushed the sheet underneath her and sat on the cold ground.

"No worries." He gave her a wink. "There's always tomorrow."

"Hmm." Moira closed her eye and turned her face to the moon, letting its light wash over her face. "I think I'm ready."

Caspian placed the blunderbuss in his lap. "Go on lass."

Moira took a deep breath. She called the beast forwards. Her transformation started.

She hissed through her teeth. She focused on the change, on embracing it. Her body broke and reformed smoothly and quickly. She felt the pull of the beast immediately. She stood and glared at Caspian.

He sat with the gun in his lap, watching her, his finger twitching near the trigger.

Moira took a step towards him.

Caspian glared back at her. He rose from the rock and

pointed the blunderbuss towards her. He walked slowly towards the broken wall, the gun held at waist-height.

She kept her mind calm and felt the creature's hunger as her own. The intense craving for flesh urged her forwards, but she just had to wait for the feeling to pass. She dug her claws into the dirt, pulling huge handfuls of earth out of the ground, then threw her head to the sky. She howled and sunk her claws back into the soil. Her claws raked through the soil. The feeling faded to sickness. She gave one final roar before she felt her two parts click together.

Moira ripped her hands from the ground and stood. Her frame rose and fell with every heavy breath.

The sensation was strange; the pull in her mind had become a push. Thoughts became instinct, her suggestions became actions. She was flooded with images, she felt desires. She struggled to make sense of it all.

"What's going on lass?" Caspian waved the blunderbuss at her. "I've got an itchy trigger finger here. If you're in there —if you've got it under control—let me know."

Moira's mouth watered at the scent of him and her claws twitched with anticipation, but she turned away. Taking several steps away from him, she reared up and howled. Her whole body shook with rage, but she kept herself in place.

Caspian leaned the blunderbuss against the wall and clapped his hands together. "I think you've got it lass."

Moira closed her eye and focused on calming herself. With one last growl, she changed back.

She lay naked on the ground. Caspian ran up to her and threw the blanket over her. Moira sat up and wrapped the sheet around her shoulders.

Crouching down beside her, Caspian wiped the tears and sweat from her face. "I would consider that a success."

Moira panted on the ground and brushed his hands away. "Hold on a bit . . . there's a lot . . . a lot of . . . everything."

"I'll give you a moment." He gave her a wink then sat back down on his rock. "Then we'll get all your things gathered up and head home. We have a lot to celebrate."

CHAPTER 24

The soft patter of rain pinged against Moira's window and the heavenly smell of buttered breads and cooked egg wafted around her.

With a stretch of her arms, she pulled herself upright. She squinted around the room for the source of the smell.

Someone had placed a desk in her room while she'd been asleep. It sat beside her with a chair tucked between its curved legs.

Resting on top of it was a plate heaped full of breakfast as well as a cup and pitcher. Next to her breakfast stood a card bent in the middle. Also resting on the desk was a quill resting in an inkwell accompanied by several sheets of parchment.

Moira struck out and snatched the card off of the desk before bouncing back down on the bed. She bent it straight and held it up to the light to read.

Moira,

Congratulations on last night. No one will be there when you wake up this morning. I've arranged for the cook to leave something for you. I have some work to do and I have something planned for this evening, but I need some time to get everything together. If you could stay in your room for a couple of hours this morning, that would be excellent. I thought you might want to spend that time writing a letter to that lad Lincoln. It won't have an address, but it will get to him eventually. Relax and sleep in a little—I'll send someone to get you when everything is ready.

Regards,
Caspian

Moira folded the card and placed it back onto the desk. She lifted herself to her feet with a grunt and pulled the chair out. She lowered herself down and pulled the plate towards her. She picked at the heap for several minutes while she listened to the gentle rain. Once she was full, Moira rose from the desk and walked over to her window, cracking it open. Drops of rain dotted the windowsill and peppered her face. She took a in a deep breath of the cool damp air and let it out with a sigh. She left the window open as she sat at the desk.

She grabbed a piece of toast and bit into the buttery, crisp bread.

"That is so good." She took another bite. "The pork was good, but what have I been missing?"

Moira stared at the inkwell as she sampled everything on her plate. She knew she wanted to tell Lincoln something, but she wasn't sure how to say it.

She shifted through the thick pieces of paper and lifted

the quill from the inkwell. Scraping the excess ink from the tip of the quill, she began to write.

Dear Lincoln,

I know it's been a long while since we've seen each other, but I wanted to say thank you for helping me that night. I know you feel guilty about what happened, but everything is all right now.

Your friend,
Moira Ashe

Moira dropped the quill back into the well and read her letter over.

She frowned. "It's a little short."

She set the letter down to dry beside the stack of paper and leaned back in her chair. "Maybe we should try writing another one?"

She picked the quill out of the inkwell again when a knock came at the door.

"Come in."

The door swung open, revealing Captain Toal. He had his hat clasped against his chest. He tilted his head towards her, revealing the patch of thinning hair at the back of his scalp.

"Caspian sent me to collect you. Are you ready to go?"

"Just about."

Moira dropped the quill back into the inkwell and picked up her letter. She gave it another read over. The ink on the paper started to run slightly downwards. She laid the letter down and blew on it. Once the ink stayed firm on the page, she gently folded the letter.

The guard at her door held his hand out to her. "I can look after that for you. I'll have it sealed and sent with one of the boats in the harbour."

Moira set the letter in his hand. "It needs to be sent to Abalon . . ."

"To a lad by the name of Lincoln Clarke, but with no specific address. Yes, Caspian told me to take care of everything once you've been escorted to him."

"And where is he exactly?"

The guard slipped the letter into his coat. "When you're ready, you'll find out. I'll be waiting outside the door." He turned and closed the door behind him.

Moira followed behind her escort as he led her through the streets of the city. Their boots squished through the mud covering the cobblestone road. The guard led her to the marketplace and continued down towards the city docks. Moira glanced around at the quiet street as she kept stride with him. The crowds, the horses, the vendors—all of it was gone. The only remnants of the market that remained were those standing ignored behind the glass of locked-down storefronts.

"Where is everyone?" Moira said.

Her escort stopped and turned to her. "Hold a second here." He popped a few beans into his mouth and chewed.

Moira stopped beside him.

The guard sent a shower of droplets dripping from the flopped edges of his hat when he swung his head to look down the street. "Do you hear it?"

Moira strained her ears against the patter of the rain. It was faint, but she heard the distant chatter.

"A crowd?"

He nodded. "Caspian has temporarily suspended all daily activities, excluding the essential workers of course, so that they can attend this event of his."

"For what?"

"For you." Her escort turned and beckoned her forwards before he continued walking down the road. "Come on, they're waiting for you."

Moira trotted up beside him. "For me? What is this all about?"

"You'll see."

He led her past the dockside wall and took her left. Farther down the street was a wall of people, all of whom were pressing and pushing to get as far down the street as possible. Others scaled the buildings around them, sitting on roofs and hanging out of windows, all looking down the street.

"Clear the way, guest of honour coming through!" the guard yelled, firing his pistol as they approached the masses.

The outer layer of people turned to them and cowered at their approach. The crowd parted quickly with a crescendo of grunts and whines as people were crushed between their neighbours. They stared at Moira as she strode through the gap.

Dozens of them glared at her.

A man from the crowd called, "Fancy clothes don't make you better than us."

Moira stopped in her tracks when a clump of mud splattered the back of her coat.

The man laughed. "Now you're just like the rest of us."

Toal pulled his club from his belt. "Motherfucker."

Some of the crowd started to bark and yell at the captain, hurling insults as he approached.

The thrower pounded a muddy fist against his chest and took a step forwards but was pulled back by the crowd.

The guard captain lashed out at the man with his fist before Moira could step between the two. "Hold it."

The thrower's nose was bent to the side and blood seeped from his nostrils. He growled and pulled hard against the hands holding him back.

Toal raised the club.

Moira grabbed the weapon. "It's just a little dirt."

Toal slid the weapon back into his belt.

"Thank you."

The other man laughed. "I know the real reason why they make your coats yellow. Coward."

Toal wiped the dirt off of Moira and led her forwards. "Come on, the stink of these lot are giving me a headache."

Moira's escort hurried her through the crowd to a line of guards that formed a buffer zone between the crowd outside and the crowds inside the square. At the centre of the square sat a large stage dominated by Caspian. Moira could hear his voice carrying over the idle chatter of the crowd. Seated in individual boxes in front of the stage was another crowd separated by a similar buffer zone of guards. They were shielded by a large tent which stretched above their seats.

Caspian spotted her from on top of the stage and pointed to her. "Is that her? Everyone! Our guest of honour is finally here."

The chatter of the crowd died down and many looked to where he pointed. As they spotted her, a wave of murmurs spread through the crowd.

Caspian waved Moira forwards. He walked to the edge of the platform. "Come on."

Moira rushed towards the base of the stage and reached

up to Caspian. He grabbed her hand and hoisted her up on stage. He then turned and faced the sea of faces looking up at him. Moira was stunned by the volume of people that stood before her. Standing in the square, hanging off of buildings, crowded in the streets leading out of the square . . . there must have been tens of thousands waiting there in the rain.

Waiting for her.

"All right my friends, I know this isn't the best weather for this and I know that some of you lads are just itching to auction off these beautiful fish of yours"—he gestured at the curtain of massive fish that hung behind them—"but there is a very special someone who I need to introduce to you."

He stepped backwards next to Moira and ushered her towards the crowd. "Many of you have probably heard stories and whispers about a new hunter—not only one who has come to protect you, the people of Trident Bay, but one who has already slain the Terror of Trident Bay."

Several whoops and cheers could be heard at the mention of the beast's death.

"I've gathered you all here today to tell you that those stories and whispers you've heard are absolutely true. That hunter is here beside me now."

Caspian pulled Moira forwards, planting her at the dead-centre of the stage. "Here she is, Moira Ashe! Let's give her a proper Trident welcome!"

The crowd clapped.

"I assure you lads and lasses, she is as deadly as she is beautiful. You know I didn't bring you all out here just to make an introduction—no my friends, absolutely not. I brought you out here for a very special reason. Commander Lynch, if you would come forwards now please," Caspian called out to the crowd.

The commander of the guard, flanked by two of his guards, stepped out onto the stage and approached Moira with a box. Caspian joined the group and nodded to the commander for the box to be opened.

The commander pulled the lid off of the box, revealing a golden Trident Bay chest pendant attached to a chain. Moira gasped at the piece of jewellery.

Caspian lifted the pendant out by the chain and let it dangle in front of Moira's eyes. "Do you know what this is lass?"

She shook her head.

He took her by the hand and led her to the edge of the platform. He then raised the pendant to the crowd, letting them marvel at the piece of jewellery.

"This pendant will represent a promise between myself, the people of Trident Bay, and its bearer. It will also grant rights and responsibilities to its wearer: the same rights and responsibilities shared by every citizen of Trident Bay." He lowered the pendant and turned to Moira, grasping her hand in his as he did so. "By my right as chieftain of Trident Bay, I have selected Moira for this honour. For ensuring the safety of the people and for her unwavering courage against our most dreaded foe, she has been deemed worthy in my eyes, and for this I will uphold my pact."

Caspian turned back to the crowd. "But this is not my decision to make alone. You have heard the stories about her, stories I assure you are true. Will the people of Trident Bay uphold their pact to her, to Moira Ashe?"

The faraway boos of the poor were drowned out by the cheers of the thousands near them.

Caspian turned back to her. "Moira, do you vow to continue to protect the best interests of the people and of my own?"

She froze.

"Do you vow?" His smile started to fade.

"Caspian, I can't st—"

"Wait," Orla called as she rushed the stage before being grabbed by a guard.

Moira felt the blood drain from her face.

Caspian whispered. "Everything is going to be fine lass." He waved to the guard. "Let her go."

Orla wiggled out of his grasp and climbed up to the top of the stage. "They're lying to you," she called out to the crowd.

The crowd went quiet.

Caspian approached her slowly. "What are you doing?"

She spat at him. "Shut up you bastard." She turned back to the crowd. "Moira is a danger to you all."

"I'm sorry things didn't work out between us Orla, but slandering Moira won't solve anything," he said, making sure his voice was loud and clear.

"This has nothing to do with us." She pointed at Moira. "That bitch is a werewolf."

Murmurs rippled through the crowd.

Caspian crossed his arms. "Prove it."

"She's wanted by Ryan Quinn."

He laughed. "I said prove it. Where's your evidence?"

"I found the wanted poster in your vest, but she tore it up."

The chatter rose in the crowd.

Caspian turned to the crowd. "People, people, I have never seen nor heard such a thing. These are clearly lies."

"No, you're lying, I had it in my hands. You have to believe me—Moira may have killed the Terror, but we're

just trading one monster for another. We need to kill her."
She pointed to the crowd. "Any one of you could be her
next victim."

Moira stood looking out at the thousands of confused
and scared people. She could feel her hand start to tremble.

"Let Moira speak," came a cry from the crowd.

Someone called from outside the square, "Kill her just
to be safe."

"Let's hear her side," cried another. "Let her defend
herself."

Many people agreed to let her speak.

Moira stepped forwards and let out a breath. "I killed
the Terror to protect the people of Trident Bay." She looked
at Orla. "For Orla to make such a horrible accusation—to
demand my death, all so she can get revenge on Caspian . .
." Moira shook her head. "I'm disgusted."

Caspian nodded. "Well said lass. All this is a sad display
to get back at me, and that is all this is."

The crowd booed and yelled profanities at Orla.

Tears cascaded from Orla's eyes. "No, you don't understand. Please, she is a monster, you are all in danger. This
has nothing to do with Caspian."

Caspian nodded to Commander Lynch. "Get her out
of here."

The commander nodded and grabbed Orla.

"No, let go." She batted her fists against him.

Moira let out a sigh as she watched the other woman
being dragged away. Orla's tear-streaked face looked back at
her, eyes full of malice.

Caspian turned to the crowd. "Let's get this ceremony
going again." He raised an eyebrow and smiled as he fixed
his gaze on someone in the crowd. "I assume no one
objects?"

"I have no objection Caspian—you'll just be adding another vicious thug to your band of thieves," Plunkett yelled as he pushed his way to the line of guards. He stood before them with his back straight and his head held high.

Caspian laughed. "Plunkett. You're a stupid bastard, aren't you? I knew you you'd show up eventually."

The guards nearest to him reached to grab him.

Several crowd members around Plunkett pulled out knives and thrust them towards the guards.

The guards readied their weapons as the crowd behind them cowered.

"People, listen to me. The blonde woman was correct about the threat of Moira Ashe. She shot two people during one of our rallies and brutalized others. I'm not sure if she really is a werewolf, but she is certainly a monster."

"The people I shot had just killed a member of the guard."

He nodded. "A guard under the employ of the infamous brute Liam Toal, sent to beat and break anyone brave enough to stand against him. Today we take back our future."

"Wait," Moira shouted. "What if you joined his council? You could bring your people's issues to the table where they can be solved."

Plunkett pointed to Caspian. "Look at the company your chieftain holds: abusers, mutilators, extortionists, murderers. I would never join such criminals."

Captain Toal walked along the line of guards and spat at Plunkett's feet. "Look at your own company Plunkett—those mongrels you call friends look ready to murder and thieve."

"Only because we've been giving no choice." He pulled

out a sword, raised it in the air and shouted, "Today the tyrant falls!"

Hundreds of men and women pulled out their weapons and assaulted Toal and his men.

The crowd screamed and ran from the violence.

Caspian placed the pendant in Moira's palm. "Time to choose Moira: are you with us or are you with them?" He pointed to the mob.

She stuffed the pendant into her pocket. "I'm with you."

He smiled and patted her on the shoulder as he drew his axe.

Moira drew hers.

They jumped off of the stage to join the defence. Dozens were dead, peasant and guard alike, by the time Moira and Caspian reached the skirmish.

Caspian yelled over the screams and cries: "Take Plunkett alive."

The guard in front of Moira collapsed in front of her, coat covered with blood. His killer yanked his dagger out of his victim and charged at her. Moira grabbed the attacker's wrist and thrust the top of her axe into his chest.

The man stumbled backwards.

Moira yanked him forwards and smashed her fist into his face.

He lashed out with his free hand but missed.

She kicked his leg, driving him to one knee, and slammed the side of her axe against the back of his head.

He fell to the ground unconscious.

A rioter beside her cried out in pain as he was impaled by a hooked spear.

Dozens of guards waded against the surge of the fleeing crowd to join the line of guardsmen.

A new attacker came at Moira, swinging a cleaver at her. She batted away the weapon with her axe.

The rioter swung again, and she batted his swing away again.

He brought the weapon above his head and chopped down at her. She held her weapon between her hands and caught the cleaver on the shaft of her weapon. She kicked him in the groin.

Her attacker groaned as he bent forwards. Moira swung her axe against his head, dropping him to the ground.

"Keep fighting," yelled Plunkett.

Moira stopped to see the man, bloody and beaten, being dragged through the guard's line by Caspian.

Caspian handed him over to two guards and then returned to re-join the fight.

"Never forget, never surrender!" cried Plunkett as he was dragged out of the square. He went limp as one of the guards smashed him over the head with the hilt of her sword.

A scream near Moira pulled her attention back to the fight.

The mob broke ranks and fled as they became outnumbered.

The guards pursued.

Rioters were tripped by the hooked spears of the guards running behind them. Others dropped to the ground beneath a hail of gunfire. Those that lived were dragged away in the same direction as Plunkett.

Caspian strode up next to her. "Damn bloody business."

The guards started piling the bodies.

Moira shook her head. "How many is that? Two hundred people dead."

He patted her shoulder. "We got Plunkett and most of his mob. The old quarter will quiet down now."

"Why did it have to come at such a cost?"

"Everything has a cost."

She crossed her arms. "Two hundred lives." She shook her head. "There must have been a better way."

He sighed. "What's done is done lass. Come on, let's get out of the city for a while, clear your head. Get some fresh air."

She nodded. "Yeah, I'd like that."

CHAPTER 25

The twilight glowed around them as they strolled through the drizzle on the edge of the forest.

"What are you going to do now that you have Plunkett?"

"The point of coming out here was to not think about that."

"How am I supposed to ignore what happened?"

Caspian smiled. "Fair enough. I'll weasel out the last of these usurpers, then Trident Bay will start to flourish again. The real question is, what are you going to do?"

"I'm going to sail to Qesuis."

He grabbed her arm. "You could stay here."

She sighed. "I can't."

"Why not? The werewolf issue is taken care of—both Orla and your control issues. You're a citizen of the city and a hero. Why not stay?"

She sighed. "I can't say I haven't thought about it."

"Do you even know where you're going after you get to Qesuis?"

"No."

"Then stay here. You'll be safe from Quinn. You can have an actual life here"

She pulled the pendant out of her pocket. "I never took the oath."

"Wearing it is enough. Here." Caspian plucked the pendant out of her hand and hooked the chain around her neck. "Now you're a citizen of Trident Bay. Congratu-lations."

She picked it off her chest and held it in front of her face. "Thank you."

"Will you stay?"

Moira sighed and pressed her back to the tree behind her. "I'll think about it." Moira kicked her heel against the wood as Caspian approached her, a smirk on his face. "What is it?"

Caspian pressed her against the damp wood with his body. He brushed her lips with his.

Moira pushed him back but kept her fingers on his heaving chest. "Right here?"

Caspian twitched his head to the side. "I can't think of anywhere better."

She pulled off her gloves, tossing them aside as Caspian pulled off her coat.

Caspian put his hands on her hips as Moira lifted her shirt over her head.

Moira laughed as Caspian pulled his vest apart, popping the buttons off the fabric. He pulled his sweater off in a single motion.

He gave her a wink as she smiled with a raised eyebrow. Moira lowered her hands onto his shoulders and ran her hands over the muscles there, heading down to his chest.

The cold of the rain did little to cool them. Moira could see the steam rising off of Caspian's skin and the vapour of their quick breaths.

Caspian pulled Moira's hat off and tossed it away. He ran his hands through her hair before he pulled her head to one side.

He pushed his chest against her and pressed his lips against her jaw, moving slowly down to her shoulder.

Moira let out a gasp as he massaged her shoulder with his mouth. She grabbed the back of his head.

Caspian pulled away from Moira

He pulled off their belts.

Moira kicked off her boots and dropped her pants.

Caspian grabbed her by the thighs and hoisted her farther up the trunk of the tree.

Moira reached up and grasped the branch as she locked her legs around his waist. Caspian squeezed her thighs and kissed her chest. She lowered one of her hands to Caspian's head and guided him over her breasts.

"Grab the branch," Caspian breathed.

Moira grabbed the limb with both hands and pulled herself higher. Caspian released her thighs and pulled at his trousers. As they fell to the ground, he grabbed hold of her again.

She lowered herself onto him. She let out a sharp breath as she sunk to his waist.

His movements were slow at first: a steady forwards and up, back and down. The movements grew faster as they found a rhythm.

Moira dropped her hands from the tree branch down to his shoulders and squeezed him closer with her legs. She dug her nails into the muscles of his shoulders as her heart beat out of her chest, as the heat burned her, as Caspian pressed her again and again against the tree behind her.

Moira raised her face to the sky. She let the rain and sweat run down her face, closing her eyes and losing herself in the rhythm of Caspian's hips.

CHAPTER 26

They awoke together.

Moira laid her head against Caspian's chest while he stroked the side of her face.

She dragged herself closer to his head and laid her chin against his shoulder. "I haven't done that in years."

Caspian raised an eyebrow with a smirk. "Was it worth the wait lass?"

Moira smiled and kissed his chest. "Worth every second."

He chuckled. "I always aim to please."

They lay there for a few hours while the sun rose behind them. Its heat warmed their bodies and dried the wet grass around them.

With a sigh, Moira pushed herself off of Caspian's chest. She rose to her feet and grabbed her pants and coat. She draped the coat over her shoulders and stepped away from Caspian, leaving him lying on the ground, completely exposed.

"Leaving so soon lass?" Caspian said as he shifted to his side.

"As happy as I would be to lie around with you until a shepherd and his flock come across us," she said as she bent down and picked up Caspian's trousers, "we have a ship to prepare."

He flinched as Moira tossed his trousers onto his crotch.

"You're not staying?"

Moira fastened her belt around the waist of her pants and turned to Caspian. "It was a nice thought, but it would never work."

"It will work."

"How?" she asked as she slid her shirt over her head.

"I'll think of something."

Moira sighed as she snatched his sweater off the ground and threw it into his chest. She then strode over to him and dropped her boots near his head. Caspian held the boots for her and slipped them onto her feet.

"It might work for a while, but I'm the famous slayer of the Terror of Trident Bay—word will spread, and what happens when Quinn comes knocking?" She looked down at him with her hands on her hips.

Caspian leaned back. He looked up at her and held out his arms. "I'll figure that out too."

She shook her head. "After what Orla said, all it would take is someone getting hold of one of those posters. Then I'd be done for—and those damn things are everywhere."

He sighed as he sat up and pulled his trousers over his legs. Moira buttoned her coat.

"Well that's it, the coat is closed. There's no hope in convincing you anymore," Caspian said. He stopped halfway through pulling his trousers up. "I'll tell the captain to get the ship ready."

Moira bent down beside him. "I'm sorry, but this is what's best for both of us."

She kissed him.

Moira rose as Caspian pushed himself to his feet. "When will the ship be ready?"

"Late this evening."

She frowned. "That late?"

"I need to arrange a few favours first." He winked, then lifted his jumper over his head. "I have to make sure you don't get shot as soon as you walk off the boat."

Moira ran her fingers over the scattered pinpricks of the scars that peppered his side. She pulled her hand away as Caspian pulled his jumper down. "I don't remember these from the first time we met."

"They were there—they're from when the Terror almost ripped my side out with his teeth."

"It doesn't look that bad though. It could have been much worse," Moira said as she rubbed her shoulder.

"Well, that root of Teague's is one hell of a miracle-worker. Hurts like a bitch though."

"Where does he get it from?"

"Teague knows the name of it, but it's somewhere far away lass, somewhere very very far away."

"Do you think I could get some?"

Caspian laughed. "Looking to pick a fight with more monsters?"

She nodded. "It's how I make a living."

He rubbed his chin. "If Teague still has the stuff, I guess I could. Consider it a going-away present."

"Will you be able to get it before I leave?"

He walked up to her and held her shoulders. "Relax and have some fun, you'll have plenty of time to get to Qesuis. Then you can fill every single one of the world's creatures with as much lead as your heart desires."

She smiled. "Do you promise?"

"I'll buy the rounds myself."

He laughed as she gave him a playful push.

"Well lass, I have a day filled with work ahead of me, what are you going to do today?"

Moira turned and scooped up her hat, placed it on her head, and began walking away from him. "I'm going to take your advice; I'm going to rest and relax."

"And what about the fun?" he called after her.

"Well, if I have so much time, I don't see why we can't have a little fun together before I leave."

CHAPTER 27

Caspian bent down and shook Moira as she lay on her back with her boots resting on the arm of his couch. She half-opened her eye and stretched. "Wake up Moira."

"Is everything ready?"

"It's still going to be a couple of hours, but I think I found a solution."

"You can get the ship ready faster?"

"No, I found a solution so you can stay."

"Caspian, we've be—"

"Hear me out first."

Moira sighed. "I'm listening."

He smiled. "We heard rumours a few days ago from travellers coming up from the south road to Quinn, so we sent a patrol to investigate."

Moira opened her eye and swung her legs down to the floor as she sat up in her seat. "What did they find?"

Caspian pulled a folded coat out from under his arm, its green fabric stained with blood.

"They pulled this off of one of the corpses." He held the coat between his hands and let the garment unfold itself as it fell open. The shoulder of the coat was almost torn completely out. Her eye widened as she saw the coat. Sickness swirled in her stomach. "That corpse was a highwayman by the name of Keegan Tait."

Moira sat with her hands wrapped around her sides. "Why are you telling me this?"

Caspian tilted his head. "Well lass, from that look on your face, I'm guessing you know something about this, and I don't know if you noticed"—he pushed his fist through the hole in the shoulder—"but I can only think of one thing that could have done this to Keegan. The same thing that tore the rest of his crew to pieces. And unless you know of any other werewolves that just recently came from that direction, that leaves you."

Moira nodded, but refused to meet his gaze. "I did it. After everything that happened in Quinn, I just lost control."

Caspian balled up the coat and tossed it away. "Don't worry about it lass, Keegan and his crew were scum. I just needed to know whether it was you or whether we had a beast stalking the roads." He stood with his hands on his hips. "But this gives me an idea."

Moira looked up to him. "What?"

"Well . . . Keegan and I had an arrangement."

"You had an arrangement with highwaymen?" Moira sighed. "I'm not surprised at this point."

Caspian raised an eyebrow. "You can tear them to pieces, but I can't make a deal with them?"

"It's not the same!" Moira glared at him. "I was alone, surrounded by men threatening me with guns—what should I have done? Let them do whatever they wanted to me? I didn't enjoy what I did—I feel sick just thinking about it." She pointed a finger at him.

"Listen lass. Bandits aren't complete idiots, they know how to hide from the guard patrols and there's too much land to search for the bastards, so I came up with a compromise. Instead of risking guards' lives hunting and fighting them, I would ally myself with a specific gang: Keegan's gang."

Moira crossed her legs and her arms and leaned back. "And what deal did you cut with this bandit?"

"He would keep the territory around the trade routes clear of the more vicious gangs and wouldn't break any of the major laws—he could rough his victims up a bit though. In exchange, his crew could operate without guard interference and would receive a bit of a payment as long as the complaints weren't too drastic."

Moira's arms fell to her side. "They weren't going to hurt me?"

"What?" Caspian reached out and grabbed her hand as he saw the colour drain from her face. "It's all right lass, you didn't know about any of this."

She stared into the void for a moment before snapping her attention back to Caspian. "I didn't need to kill them."

"You didn't know that."

"I could have just left . . ."

Caspian wiped the tear from her cheek. "It's all right Moira, you did the right thing."

They sat in silence for several seconds before Moira took a deep breath. She cleared her throat and took another heavy breath. "How does any of this help me stay here?"

"Since you seem to have that whole werewolf thing under control now, I was thinking that you could take over the territory yourself."

"You want me to live outside the city walls?"

"Not for long lass. Once word spreads that a werewolf is

tearing every bandit in the area to pieces, they'll eventually leave the area alone. A few gangs will try to press into the area after a while, but once you take care of them, you'll get a break for a good while before the next bastard tries again."

"What happens when everyone puts Orla's accusation and these werewolf sightings together?"

Caspian clapped his hands together. "That's the beauty of it. We tell them ourselves."

Moira leapt to her feet. "Are you insane?"

He shook his head. "If we explain to them that you won't hurt them, that you're keeping the roads safe—"

"Hunters would come to kill me."

He shook his head. "A few hunters might show up for the challenge, but no one will care if a few bandits are found dead."

"And what will we do when those hunters show up?" Moira felt her heart beat faster in her chest and her thoughts go wild.

Caspian squeezed her hand. "We'll take care of them together."

She lifted the pendant up to her face and stared at the shimmering golden crest for a moment before closing her eye. She let the pendant drop back to her chest with a sigh and opened her eye to look at Caspian. "I can't do it. I'm leaving so I don't kill anyone else."

"They're bandits."

"They're still people."

Caspian frowned as his shoulder sagged. "I understand."

"Why do you want me to stay so badly?"

"I meant it when I said you were special. For so long, I've been surrounded by all of these people who were only out for themselves, always looking for an opportunity to profit off someone else's failure." He grabbed her shoulders. "Then you came along: beautiful, incredibly strong, looking out for everyone's wellbeing. I want you to stay not just for me, but for this city. We need people like you."

"People like what?"

"People willing to sacrifice for the greater good, people like me and you, the kind of people who get things done."

Moira frowned. "I'm sorry, but I can't stay." She placed a hand against his cheek. "But we could leave together."

He laughed. "I'm tempted, but this place would fall to pieces without me, and I've sacrificed too much to let that happen."

She dropped her hand "So this is the end."

"Not quite yet." He smirked. "We still have several hours. My bed is upstairs, and I remember you saying something about having some fun before you leave."

Moira smiled. "I remember that too." She took his hand and led him to the stairs.

CHAPTER 28

Moira smiled as she rested her head on Caspian's chest.

He was asleep. His chest rose and fell in his peaceful slumber. She laid her hand on his chest and pressed her ear against his chest. She closed her eye and lay beside him, listening to the air enter and exit his lungs and the powerful pulse of his heart.

She touched the scars on his chest and ran her fingers down the path carved by the Terror's claws. Caspian's body had taken an incredible amount of punishment over the years.

Moira ran her fingers over his skin, seeking out the various scars scattered across him.

A mass of scars cut into his forearm and the palm of his hand. She found slivers etched into his sides, as well as pinpricks dotting his shoulders.

As she slid her hand over the collection of circular marks left on his side, she continued across his stomach. She froze as her hand found another scar.

She opened her eye and leaned over Caspian's body to

look at it. It was located on the other side of his abdomen, far from the others. She looked at Caspian's face as she shifted herself closer to him, then lightly touched one of his scars. There was still no response from him.

Moira turned her attention back to the scars. The lone scar nagged at her thoughts. If the Terror's teeth had made the other scars, where had this one come from?

She ran her fingers over the scars on his side. They were too scattered to be from a set of jaws, even those of a creature with as many teeth as the Terror. The scars were circular dots, not long and ragged.

Moira withdrew her hand and stared at the scars. If they hadn't been caused by teeth, what had caused them?

Bullets.

She felt a pit form in the bottom of her stomach. Why would he lie?

But when did he get shot?

She looked into the peaceful face of Caspian and wondered at the possibilities.

She pulled her hand away from him as a thought crossed her mind.

The scars on his forearm and hand, the scars on his side —all were places she'd inflicted wounds on the Terror.

But the Terror was dead.

There had to be another explanation for all of this; the scars had to be a coincidence. She thought back to her fights with the Terror and ran it all back through her head.

She remembered the number of times she'd stabbed the beast's face and neck.

Moira pulled herself farther up the bed and tilted to see Caspian's nose.

She spotted a cut hidden in the crevice of his nose.

She ran her hand across the other side of his neck.

Caspian's eyes opened.

He squinted through his tired eyes. "What time is it?"

She stared at him. Her mouth moved but she didn't know what to say. Should she ask him? Accuse him to his face? Report him? Who would she even report him to?

He raised an eyebrow. "Are you all right Moira?"

"I'm all right. It's still only early evening."

Caspian stretched out his arms and arched his back. He leaned back and watched Moira as she swung out of bed and grabbed her clothes off the floor.

Moira pulled on her clothes and stood at the foot of the bed with her coat in her hand. "Where is the ship docked?"

Caspian sighed. "There is no ship."

She gripped the coat tight. "What?"

He shook his head. "No ship is going to take you to Qesuis."

"But I held up my end of the bargain. I even told you about the meeting with Gaspard."

"I know, but I couldn't get the restrictions lifted for you. If you take one step in Qesuis, you'll be arrested and executed."

She threw the coat at him. "You only tell me this now?"

He stood up from the bed with his hands held towards her. "I wanted to convince you to stay so you wouldn't have to worry about it."

Moira shook her head as she put her hands on her hips. "I don't believe this." She pointed a finger at him. "I don't believe you."

"It's the truth."

"Bullshit." She ripped the hat off of her head and threw it at him. "This is because I won't stay, isn't it? You're forcing me to stay."

"I still need you to help me snuff out Gaspard." He took a step towards her.

She slapped him. "Fuck off." She opened the door. "You're not going to keep me here. I'll find a way out." She yanked the necklace off her neck and threw it into his chest. "I'm sure Gaspard will be able to get me there." She spat the words at him as he bent down to pluck the pendant off the ground.

She saw the scar on his shoulder—it was in the same place as the wound she'd inflicted on the Terror. The thought made her sick.

Moira slammed the door behind her, grabbed her gear, pulled on her old coat, placed her tricorn on her head, and walked out of Caspian's house.

CHAPTER 29

M oira stood in front of Gaspard's violet-coloured estate and knocked on the front door.

A servant answered the door. "Who are you mademoiselle? And why are you bothering the estate of Gaspard Proulx the third?"

"I'm Moira Ashe. Gaspard knows me." The words seemed to stick in her throat. "I've come to speak with Gaspard about urgent business."

"I will see if he will accept you. Wait here." The servant closed the door behind him. After a few minutes, he opened the door for her and gestured for her to enter.

"This way mademoiselle."

He led her to a room to the left.

"Monsieur Proulx. I present Mademoiselle Ashe."

Gaspard waved him away and raised a goblet to his lips. "Would you care for a drink?" He gestured to an open bottle of wine on the table in front of him.

Moira shook her head.

"Although I am glad to speak with you again, I must inform you that your visit is bound to raise some questions."

"Caspian already knows you're conspiring against him."

Gaspard lowered the goblet. "Is that so?" He cleared his throat. "Is that why you came here?"

"I need your help getting to Qesuis."

"Is that what Caspian promised you?"

Moira frowned.

Gaspard smirked. "I figured as much." He pointed to her clothes. "That's the only reason you'd put on such a dreadful garment."

"Can you help me?"

"Of course I can, but what are you going to do for me in return?"

She narrowed her eye at him. "Depends on what you want."

Gaspard placed the goblet on a tray next to the bottle. "I want you to kill Caspian."

She crossed her arms and shook her head. "Absolutely not."

"Then our business is concluded." He turned his head away and waved her off. "Leave me."

She turned to leave Gaspard's house, then turned back. "Will you answer a question for me?"

"Why do I want Caspian dead?"

"No, I know why. I want to know if Caspian was at a council meeting when I set sail with *The Fortune's Tide*."

"*The Fortune's Tide?* Alistair Sand's ship. I don't believe he was; Captain Toal dropped off a list of his orders that day." Gaspard scoffed. "Hardly unusual for the fishmonger."

She left Gaspard's house, the sickness in her gut worsening.

. . .

Moira placed her hands on her forehead and swore. She needed a way out that didn't involve her killing more people.

She paced back and forth as she tried to think of what to do, but her thoughts kept turning to Caspian's scars and his whereabouts during her voyage.

It would certainly explain how Caspian knew so much about the beast inside her; he had his own.

She stopped. She had no idea how to find a way to Qesuis right now, but she knew someone who could answer her questions about Caspian.

Moira strode off to the Apothecary's End.

CHAPTER 30

M oira stepped into the stale and musky air of Teague's shop.

"Teague? Are you here? Teague? I need you to answer some questions for me."

She spun around as she searched the room, peering around the piles of books and jars.

"Teague?"

"The only questions I answer are my own."

Teague materialized in front of her through a pair of drapes which hid a door in the corner of the room. He strode to the back of the table in the centre of the room and leaned over it, studying Moira through his mask.

"Why are you here?"

"I have some questions about siorclans."

"Hmmm, a curious topic." He scratched the bottom of his mask with a gloved hand. "Why ask me?"

She looked around the shop. "You seem the curious sort. I'm guessing you would want to know about such a beast."

He bobbed his head. "Indeed, but you are the hunter here, not I. Surely you would know more about creatures than I?" He scratched the top of his mask's beak. "After all, you did slay such a creature."

"I might experience fighting siorclans, but that isn't what I'm looking for."

He tilted his head. "Then what are you looking for?"

"Are siorclans human?"

Moira saw the apothecary's eyebrows rise under the shadow of his mask.

"What a curious question. Are siorclans human?" He stood up and paced around the room. "But what do you mean by 'human'? There are other monsters which were once human—vampires, for example. Then you have creatures that are occasionally human, like a werewolf." He put a hand into his robes. "Which is it?"

"Occasional."

"Interesting choice." He moved around the counter to stand near the door. "Well then. In your experience, did the Terror fight like a dumb beast or did it fight like something . . . more?"

She crossed her arms. "Do you know the answer or not?"

Teague tapped the bottom of his mask. "Perhaps, but I think you already know the answer yourself. Tell me your answer. Was it a dumb beast?"

Moira sighed as she leaned against the bookshelf behind her. "A bit of both I think."

"Part man, part beast. You have your answer." He walked towards the curtains.

"What do you do for Caspian?"

Teague stopped and spoke over his shoulder. "That is between Caspian and myself." He walked forwards.

Moira pointed to the shelf with the hidden back. "I know that he pays you to acquire all of these things and that he supplied you with a corpse. But are you the one who heals him when he gets injured?"

He stopped short of the curtains. "That is only a minor aspect of our business together." He turned around. "A business that is none of your concern." He stepped backwards and disappeared behind the curtain.

"Wait." Moira rushed forwards and drew back the curtain.

There was nothing there; only a small closet.

Moira swore and let the curtain fall back. If Teague knew something, he wasn't about to tell her.

She left the store and headed to the Windwake. The sun was going down and she needed somewhere to sleep.

CHAPTER 31

M oira shoved her way through the doors of the Windwake and strode up to the front counter.

"I need a room," she said, dropping a bag of coins onto the counter.

The bartender nodded and slipped a key across the counter. "Room twenty-three."

Moira gripped the key in her hand and made for the stairs. She spotted Orla staring at her as she strode by. Moira looked back out of the corner of her eye, seeing the confusion on the blonde serving girl's face and the malice burning in her brown eyes. She turned her back on Orla as she went up the stairs. She followed the hall, counting down the numbers on the doors lining either side until she came to door twenty-three.

Moira unlocked the door and stepped through. She kicked the door closed behind her and collapsed onto the bed. The musk of the room filled her nostrils with every slow breath as she stared up at the ceiling for what felt like an eternity.

The only indicators that any time had passed by were

the sounds that filtered through the walls of her room. The patter of rain began sounding on her window, granting a consistent backdrop to the muffled voices and footsteps that passed by her door and rose from outside of her window. The darkness crept slowly across the ceiling as Moira tried to make sense of it all.

She rubbed her eye with a sigh.

How could she get to Qesuis?

Were Caspian and the Terror one and the same?

If so, would he continue to kill?

Would she kill him? Should she? Her situation was different to his after all.

Her eye slowly closed as she drifted to sleep.

The click of the door closing woke her.

Moira sprung into a sitting position and gasped as she saw the flourish of blonde strands and the flash of sharpened steel.

She grabbed the blade of the kitchen knife as Orla leapt on top of her, driving Moira onto her back. Orla kept her eyes pinned to Moira's face, while Moira kept her eye focused on the tip quivering an inch from her heart. The serving girl threw all of her weight onto the hilt of the weapon, slicing into the leather of Moira's gloves and driving it closer to her chest. Moira's arms shook from the strain of holding the other woman up by the edge of the blade. Moira's grip slipped and the weapon slipped forwards, sinking into her skin.

With a roar of pain and effort, Moira pulled her legs under Orla and up towards her chest. She kicked out, driving her attacker against the door.

Moira scrambled to her feet and brought her hands up in defence. Orla pushed herself off of the door and brandished the knife in front of her.

Not taking her eye off of Orla, Moira reached to her chest and touched her wound. She winced in pain and held her fingers to the light. A small patch of red could be seen in the faint light.

Orla pointed at her chest with the knife. "They don't believe me, none of them do, but I won't let you hurt anyone."

Eyes wild, she let out a scream as she lunged at Moira.

Moira jumped back out of the way of the blade and pulled her own knife out. "I haven't hurt anyone Orla, and I don't want to hurt you."

The blonde snapped, "You bitch, you already ruined my life." She slashed but Moira blocked it with her own weapon. "I won't let you ruin anyone else's." She slashed at her two more times but missed as Moira stepped back out of her reach. "You're not a hero." Orla lunged forwards with the knife.

Moira slashed at Orla's wrist, slicing a crimson streak across her arm.

The other woman yelped and dropped her weapon as she clutched her cut. She held it up to Moira "This is what you do, monster! You hurt people." She sobbed as Moira kicked her knife under the bed.

"It's over Orla, just leave."

"You're not a hero!" Orla screamed.

"I'm leaving Trident Bay Orla, and I'm not with Caspian."

Orla dropped her clenched fists to her side and let the blood run off of her arm and to the floor.

Moira stepped forwards.

Orla lunged at Moira and grabbed for her gun. "You're lying, just like you lied at the ceremony."

Moira growled and grabbed the barrel of the pistol with one hand while she held her knife in the other.

Orla twisted the barrel of the pistol towards Moira with both hands.

Moira drove the knife into her chest.

Orla let go of the pistol and drove her nails into the shoulders of Moira's coat as the knife plunged into her chest.

Orla tried once more to point the pistol towards Moira. She squealed through her teeth as Moira pulled the blade out and plunged it back into her.

"You couldn't have just left me alone." Moira pulled the knife out and stared at the pain in the blonde girl's eyes. Orla began to sag, pulling Moira towards the ground as her legs began to fail.

"You're . . . a . . . monster," Orla whined through blood-stained teeth. She coughed a crimson mist into Moira's face before she fell to the floor. Her tear-filled eyes glazed over as she hit the floor.

Moira breathed heavily as she stood above Orla's corpse. Blood covered the blade in her hand and soaked her gloves. She wiped the blood from her face with the back of her sleeve. Wiping the blade on Orla's dress, Moira put away her knife.

She stared at the corpse, shaking her head.

No way out of Fotland, and now a dead woman in her room.

Moira picked up her pistol, stepped over Orla, and fled the room.

CHAPTER 32

E verything only got worse as Moira walked out of the inn.

Screams echoed though the docks as droves of people ran to the city, guards included.

A roar tore through the night, spurring the crowd to flee faster.

Moira froze as she heard the call of the siorclan. She pulled out her axe and listened.

Another roar echoed. The centre dock.

She sprinted against the tide of runners, weapon gripped tight in her hands.

The beast was standing on the deck of *The Fortune's Tide*. Corpses were strewn around it.

Alistair was standing before the creature, sword drawn, hook at the ready.

Moira drew her pistol and fired it into the creature.

It roared as Alistair turned to her. "Moira."

She drew her next pistol and fired at the beast again.

Alistair slashed with his sword.

The bullet pierced the siorclan's shoulder, spraying the

creature's face with its own blood while the sword bit deep into the creature's chest.

The Terror slammed Alistair into the deck of his ship.

Moira hopped onto the deck as the creature opened its jaws.

Alistair kicked and yelled at the beast.

Snapping its jaws closed, the beast shredded through Alistair's legs. Alistair cried as he cut and slashed at the beast.

Moira raised her axe to strike while she charged forwards.

The Terror yanked Alistair backwards towards the broken piece of railing.

"Help me Moira!" Alistair pleaded as he dug at the deck with his hook and hand.

But she was too slow.

The siorclan leapt off of the ship with Alistair in tow, the man's hook stuck in the wood. He plunged screaming into the water.

"No!" Moira yelled as they disappeared.

She slammed into the railing of the ship and looked into the water.

There was nothing.

Moira yelled and smashed her axe into the mast of the ship, chopping out large splinters of wood with each swing.

She lowered her axe but kept a tight grip on the weapon. After several deep breaths, she snatched the hook from the ground.

If Caspian was the Terror, he was injured now, and she knew exactly where he would go next.

CHAPTER 33

The market district was quiet. Moira hid amongst the shadows across from the Apothecary's End, clutching her axe in one hand and Alistair's hook in the other.

A warm glow radiated from the windows of the shop.

Three figures rushed up the road towards the shop. Two were in guard uniforms and carried the third, who was draped in a brown cloak.

One guard carried the cloaked figure up the stairs and into the shop, while the other stood watch near the door.

Moira strode forwards.

The guard spotted her and held out his palm. "Hold it."

She didn't stop.

"Are you deaf? I said stop." He grabbed the pistol from his belt.

Moira swung the blunt side of her axe and smashed the side of his head. The guard stumbled. "Fuck."

Moira smashed the hook into his head twice before the guard fell to the ground. She climbed the stairs and, using her axe, chopped the wood surrounding the lock free. She kicked the door open.

The shop was empty.

She strode to the closet and pulled back the curtain. She could hear muffled voices coming from behind the wall.

Moira tapped the head of her axe against the wall. It was hollow.

She chopped through the wood with her axe.

The scent of dirt and smoke wafted through the hole left by her axe.

"What the fuck?" Captain Toal appeared at the bottom of a set of stairs that led up to Moira. He pulled out his pistol. "Moira is chopping her way in here."

"Wait, Toal," Caspian said.

He pulled the hammer back as Moira kicked her way through the wall.

"Stop Toal! If you fire that pistol I'll kill you myself."

The guard captain lifted his finger off the trigger and pointed it at the ceiling. He backed up into the corner to let her past.

The basement was filled with flesh. Jars filled with various limbs and organs lined the walls. Some parts looked human, while others were from siorclans. Half a dozen of the creature's heads lined the walls.

Caspian sat on a table in the centre of the room, hunched over and naked. He sweated and grit his teeth as wisps of smoke rose from the fresh wounds along his shoulder.

Teague was behind him, bowl in hand, smearing the crimson paste on a stab wound in his back. Once he was done, he rushed amongst the various jars and pieces of paper that covered the room and packed away those he selected.

Caspian gritted his teeth. "If you're here Moira, I guess

you know my secret. Nice shots by the way." He tried to laugh, but it turned to a growl as the paste burned his flesh.

Moira stepped forwards, her hands tight around her weapon and Alistair's hook. "I know you're the Terror of Trident Bay."

He nodded and held his breath as his skin fused together. He let out a long slow breath. "I'm the Terror of Trident Bay."

Moira felt faint as the words struck her. She felt sick to her stomach and her vision blurred from the tears welling up in her eyes. She felt confused, angry. Her whole body shook.

Caspian looked at the other two men in the room. "Leave us."

Toal tapped a finger against his pistol. "Is that a good idea boss?"

"Leave."

The captain shrugged and ascended the stairs. The apothecary stopped at the bottom of the steps, a large box in his hands. "This will be the end of our partnership Caspian." He hopped up the stairs.

"Bloody fucking Teague." Caspian shook his head. "Please, Moira, let me explain." He ran his hand over his head and took a breath. "I was given the gift by the mermaid who saved me. I don't know why—she must have seen the potential in me, but she kissed me and my life was changed forever."

"How the hell is this a gift?"

"It gave me the power to change not just my life, but the lives of everyone around me."

"But you've killed so many people Caspian."

"Only the ones that I needed to."

"The ones that you needed to? Why did you need to kill anyone?"

He crossed his arms. "I've told you that death can bring opportunities. This is what I was talking about."

"What about me? You tried to kill me twice. Is the world better off without me?"

"I'm sorry, but it was self-preservation. You were a hunter, come to kill me like all the rest. I only did what you would have done."

"I didn't come here to kill you. I came to get the hell out of here. You could have just let me leave."

"Better safe than sorry."

Moira sneered. "It almost cost you your life."

Caspian chuckled. "That it did, but I gained something so much more." He reached over the table to grab her hand. Moira withdrew from his touch. "I meant what I said Moira, every word of it. You can still have a place here with me."

"I want to leave to stop killing people. You're a mass murderer, Caspian. I can't be with someone like that."

"Well then Moira, if you think you're right"—Caspian clenched his fists—"then why am I the chieftain of a county, the owner of one of the largest businesses in Fotland? I've helped thousands. And why is it that you have barely anything to your name? Why is it? We've both killed more than our fair share of people."

"I did it to protect the lives of the people they would have killed!"

Caspian clapped. "And how did those people repay you again? You're hunted by the people you helped while I'm celebrated in the streets. Which of us is right?"

Moira stood speechless.

"Well lass?"

Moira closed her eye. "I don't know."

They sat in silence for several seconds until Moira spoke again. "What is all of this?"

"It's a whole lot of nothing. Especially now Teague is gone." He sighed as he looked at all of the jars. "What tipped you off to me?"

"The scars, and Gaspard said you were absent from that meeting."

Caspian looked down at his chest and nodded. "You spoke to Gaspard."

She nodded.

"Will he help you out of Fotland?"

"Only if I kill you."

"Will you?"

She shook. "I don't want to Caspian, but you aren't going to stop." She lifted the hook. "And I need out."

"No, you don't."

"I killed Orla, Caspian. She attacked me in my room at the Windwake and I killed her. I need to leave—now."

He stared forwards for a few seconds before nodding. "If you kill me now, you won't make it three feet out the door. Make whatever arrangements you need to with Gaspard and then met me in Lane's Folly. If we're going to do this, we need somewhere private." He stood from the table and draped the cloak over himself. He walked past Moira and up the stairs.

CHAPTER 34

The deal was struck.

Moira stood in front of the memorial with Alistair's hook in her hands. The metal of the hook glimmered in the light of the rising sun.

Her stomach turned as she looked up at all of the trinkets pinned to the board, hung for everyone to see. Like trophies.

The hat of the Quinn guard. The patch of Commander Gallagher, whose wife and children visited the memorial every day. Kevin Corcoran's crew.

She tightened her grip on the hook.

Alistair Sand and his crew.

These weren't random tragedies; each was a deliberate murder. Hundreds butchered to uphold Caspian's glory.

And he wouldn't stop.

But would she stop? Even if she did get to Qesuis, would the death end? Or was she stuck in the same cycle as Caspian, doomed to end life until her own life ended?

Was she any better than him? Caspian may have built

his accomplishments on a pile of corpses, but he had at least built something. She'd built nothing on hers.

Moira shook the thoughts from her head. Caspian needed to be stopped and, if she succeeded, she would be free.

She had no other choice.

With a grunt of effort, Moira drove the hook into the memorial, leaving it hang with the rest of Caspian's trophies. She turned and left for Lane's Folly.

CHAPTER 35

Moira found Caspian bare-chested. He'd been waiting for her.

She stopped a few paces away from him. "This is where we first fought."

"I thought it would be a fitting place for us to have our last battle. But if I talk, will you listen?"

Moira crossed her arms. "I will, but it won't change anything."

"Listen lass, I've only done what was necessary to protect the prosperity of the people."

"You killed those people for yourself."

"I did it for the people."

"Then why kill Alistair? What benefit did his death bring to the people?"

"He was taking my shipping contracts, weakening the very core of our prosperity."

"And what about your old commander of the guard? You could have just relieved him of his post."

"Old commander? Rowan Gallagher? I didn't kill him just because he was trying to kill me, lass; he was a revolution sympathiser. He was trying to harass the Qesuis nobility into leaving the city."

"What about his wife and kids?"

Caspian paused for a moment. "His wife and kids are being looked after."

"They don't need your money; they need their father. You don't care about the lives of these people. You kill because it serves you. You kill because you like doing it."

Caspian threw out his arms. "I built Trident Bay into the greatest city in Fotland. I've raised a hundred thousand people out of poverty through what I've done. You didn't see what Trident Bay was before I raised it up. You don't understand."

"And that's all it is to you: an achievement, a trophy too big to nail to your wall. I don't want to be another trophy."

"I killed for you, I helped you control the beast inside you. I've done more for you than anyone else has."

"Only because you needed me to get at Plunkett. Only because you wanted to use me."

"We can still forget about all of this. I understand you better than anyone. I can figure this out, Moira. I just need time."

"I understand, Caspian, I really do, but that money isn't going to ease all the pain you've caused. You need to be stopped. I have no other choice."

Caspian sighed. "There's no way to convince you then?"

Moira shook her head. "I need to be free, Caspian."

He nodded. "I understand."

They stood staring at each other for several seconds.

"Well then lass. How do you want to play this? A monster-to-monster fight to the death?"

Moira shook her head. "Neither of us would leave this place alive in that battle."

"Are you sure? I've seen how fast you heal."

"I can't regenerate arms, and I have no interest in losing any to those jaws of yours."

"Regular old weapons it is then." He pulled his axe from his belt. "No bullets?"

Moira pulled out her own axe. "No bullets."

They approached each other. Moira held her axe to the side while Caspian held his over his head.

They circled around the sandbar stretched across the cavern. Caspian's arms tensed and relaxed as he shifted his aim.

She stared into his dark eyes. He was begging her to strike first—so she did.

Moira swung at his chest. Caspian dodged to the side and brought his weapon down towards her back. Moira rolled forwards underneath his swing. They turned to face each other again as sand cascaded off Moira's back.

Caspian spun the weapon above his head and approached Moira. She held her ground and waited for his attack. He chopped at her from an angle; she blocked the blow with the shaft of her axe, feeling the wood split. He gave her a swift kick to the chest, causing her to lose her grip and stagger backwards.

The pieces of her weapon fell into the sand as Moira struggled for breath.

"I'm sorry," Caspian said.

Moira opened her coat and pulled out her knives. Caspian readied his weapon again as she approached.

He hopped out of reach of her first thrust and batted away her follow-up slash. Caspian then struck out with his empty hand, catching her in the chest.

Moira coughed and struggled for breath but refused to stop fighting. She slashed at his arm in retaliation and sliced a thin line into his skin. Caspian flinched at the wound and swung his axe towards her. She leaned out of the way and took a step back to avoid his follow-up swing. He then raised the weapon above his head and brought it down above her. She sidestepped his chop and slashed his sides before kicking him aside.

He smiled as he saw the crimson line across his side. "That's first blood." He twirled his axe. "Let's see who gets second."

Moira lashed out with a fury of slashes. Caspian stepped backwards as he dodged and batted away her blades. He swung at her from her left. She turned her head and ducked to dodge the axe. As she lowered herself, Caspian kicked her. She fell onto her back, clutching her knives.

Caspian hollered. "Moira, don't you just love that fire in your blood?" He twirled his axe. "Come on lass, get to your feet."

Moira got to her feet and breathed heavily as she faced Caspian. She thrust at him again. He caught her by the wrist and twisted it. She gasped as she bent forwards and her blade dropped from her hand. Caspian kicked her away.

He pounded his chest. "Come on lass, you have to do better than this."

Moira staggered back into a fighting stance.

Caspian kicked her knife at her as he surged towards her.

Moira kept her eye on Caspian and side-stepped the knife.

He swung at her but Moira grabbed the shaft of his axe.

He pulled her towards him and slammed his forehead into her nose.

Moira staggered backwards, her vision blurred.

With a swing of his axe, he knocked Moira's knife out of her hand.

He held his axe out to his side. "That's it. I win."

Moira moved towards the tunnel that led to the cliff. "Not yet."

He looked around. "You have no weapons—you're done, Moira. Just give up."

She backed up into the tunnel. Caspain sighed and followed, spinning his axe. "Fine then."

Moira searched through the water with her feet as Caspian approached her.

Her foot snagged something.

She bent over and fished her blunderbuss from the water.

"What are you doing?"

Moira turned, leapt forwards, and drove him to the ground.

Caspian dropped his axe into the water and grabbed the barrel of the gun with both hands. He grunted with effort as he strained against her weight, the tip of the bayonet pricking his skin. Moira placed all of her weight on top of the blunderbuss.

Caspian twisted the weapon sideways, causing Moira to crash down on top of him. With a yell, he threw her over him. Moira landed behind him, blunderbuss in her hands.

They both scrambled to their feet and stared at each other as their chests heaved.

Caspian bolted for his axe, but Moira was closer. She ran over and snatched the weapon off the ground with her free hand. He backed away into the tunnel.

"Come on lass, you don't have to do this."

She shook her head and moved towards him. "I have to."

"We both want what's best for everyone."

"That's why I can't let you keep terrorizing these people."

They continued to walk through the tunnel. Moira slipped the axe into her belt and looped her gun over her shoulder.

"If you kill me, everything I worked to build, everything those people were sacrificed for—it all falls apart. Look at what's happening here. Do you think Gaspard is going to do any better? He's a murderer too—the only difference is I'm willing to do the killing myself. Trident Bay won't survive without me. No one else is strong enough to keep it together."

The light of day glowed behind Caspian from a tunnel entrance around the corner.

"We can clean up the whole mess with Orla and I can keep you safe from Quinn. We're the same Moira—we can work this out."

"We may both be killers," shouted Moira, "but we don't do it for the same reasons. We may both be monsters, but I never considered it a gift. Don't you dare say that we're the same."

"I don't want to fight you Moira. This doesn't have to end this way."

"It has to, Caspian."

"I'm sorry, but I can't let all of my sacrifice be for nothing."

He bolted around the corner. Moira drew her pistols and turned the corner. Caspian was splashing the walls with every hurried footstep as he ran towards the hole in the side of the cliff.

Moira pointed the pistols at him.

She pulled the triggers.

Blood exploded out of Caspian's back as he stumbled forwards. He tripped and stumbled out of the tunnel and over the cliff.

Moira lowered the pistols. She choked back tears.

She turned away and headed to meet with Gaspard.

CHAPTER 36

Moira shielded her eyes as she walked out into the morning light.

Kevin sat on the rock bearing the scrawled depiction of the Terror. A tall bottle of wine in hand, he nodded at Moira. "Is it done?"

She nodded.

"Good riddance." He took a swig from the bottle and then held a piece of paper out to Moira. "Gaspard said to give you this. It'll get you a ride on the *Ruby Dawn*."

Moira snatched the paper out of the fisherman's hand as she walked past him.

He called after her. "You did the right thing, lass."

Moira kept walking.

CHAPTER 37

M oira approached the city gate with her shoulders hung low.

Two dozen Trident Bay guards crowded around the rickety guard post. Two horse-drawn carriages and four carts were being loaded up with men and supplies. She passed them.

"Moira?"

She turned towards her caller and froze as she saw him.

His cleanshaven face was covered with scruff, an officer's sword hung from his belt, and a captain's badge was stitched into his ragged green coat. He was perched upon a white steed.

She unslung her blunderbuss and aimed it at Flynn.

He only got halfway to pulling out his pistol before he froze.

The yellow-clad guards were stunned by the spectacle.

Moira held her finger near the trigger of her weapon as she looked into the Quinn guard's eyes. His horse paced underneath him.

She shook her head and turned her back on him as she tossed her gun to the ground.

Too many people had died already—she wasn't going to add any more.

"Do it Flynn, just do it," she said over her shoulder as she walked away. "I can't do this anymore."

Flynn took his pistol out and pointed it at her.

She closed her eye and took a deep breath as she waited for the bullet.

She opened her eye as she heard a clang. She turned and found Flynn's pistol lying at his horse's feet. She looked up to find him with his hand on his forehead.

"For fuck's sake Moira." He let out a breath. "I need your help."

www.ingramcontent.com/pod-product-compliance
Lightning Source LLC
Chambersburg PA
CBHW031422250626
47155CB00004B/1588